Wake up, We're here

Wake up, We're here

Ann Malone

© 2012 Ann Malone

Herstellung und Verlag: Books on Demand GmbH, Norderstedt.

ISBN: 9783848204106

Bibliografische Information der Deutschen Nationalbibliothek

Acknowledgements

Thank you to my family and friends who have molded me and influenced me in so many ways. Thank you for all the love and understanding I have received over all the years.

Thank you to each person who completed a form for this book, who related their stories, shared their joys and pain, people from around the globe who have settled in European cities, representing 18 nationalities and 12 religions with an age range from 15 to 80 years. Each has shared their humanity which we can all relate to.

Thank you in particular to Christian who organized his secondary school class to fill out and return forms, to Verena and Alex who collected information from several people where they work, to Fidelma and Fiona who forwarded the forms to many people, to Ximena, Marianne, Sara and Carmen who actively discussed my ideas and helped me to develop them.

Thank you Marcello, for reading the book and for your positive feedback. I wasn't sure how men would like this book. I collected so many forms from men and was eager that they could also relate to the stories. Many of my closest friends are men and no matter what women think, I know them to be just as emotional as us women folk but they may not express it openly in tears. My dear sister, Trish not only read my first draft and encouraged me but gave me great help with improving the book, preparing the cover and never giving up her belief in me. Thank you so much.

Thank you to my husband Rolf and my girls, Molly and Emma for their constant supply of love, support, inspiration and understanding in my life.

This book is dedicated to all neighborhoods like our own where people from all over the world live together in peace. The more neighborhoods like ours that survive in the world, the more we will learn how lucky we are to have each other. Good friends and family of all the colours of the rainbow making the planet a richer and fuller place. The rainforests, the richest places on earth haven't only a few types of trees and all in straight lines. Each tree, plant, animal finds its niche and thrives, nourishing and being nourished over generations. Nature is all encompassing and beautiful because of it.

The idea for this book stems from my afternoons with 5 women in particular, Anita, Eli, Gulcin, Shahnez and Ximena. As we played with our kids, discussed our pasts, our present and our hopes I realized how similar we were despite large differences in background. 6 Nations; Bolivia, Iran, Ireland, Mexico, Switzerland and Turkey all under the one roof. We have been friends over the past 10 years, with our children playing and fighting together in the playground below. We are all the wiser and happier for knowing each other. Thank you.

Please don't feel exposed if you think one of the stories is yours. You may think the details aren't quite right. You may feel that's not really the way it is or was. Well the truth is, it may be your story but it maybe thousands of others as well. The details

will vary but the emotion may be the same. It is the
emotion that binds us together. There are so many
people out there with your story.
So many people have encouraged me to finish this
book I hope you enjoy reading it at long last.

Introduction

What are we like? Here we are all sitting on the same planet, floating around in space, in oblivion. We are the ones with the big brains. That is what they tell us. And what do we use our big brains for? We set up barriers for ourselves. We are all humans and all need this planet to survive. So if we could pull together and realize that each of us has as much right to a decent meal and an easy going family life, life would be a lot easier. The majority of people want to get on with life, get the food on the table, have a roof over their heads, try to keep the people closest to them happy and stay alive.

We are as varied as the animals on the planet, each with our own capabilities, strengths and weaknesses. Despite all the labeling that we put on ourselves with religion, culture and colour, we all need to be nourished to live. We all crave a bit of love and understanding from the softest of us to the hardest of us.

I have collected the memories good and bad from people of many different nations and presented them as one life. Our life as a human. Our life striving to survive when we are lonely, hurt and sad. Our life when we are dancing and singing and hugging.

I hope that each person on this planet can identify with at least one story in this small book. And can gain understanding that maybe the person beside them is feeling the same and reacts in a totally different way because that is all that they can do. We are all individuals but we need each other. Our actions, whether good or bad, have an influence on those around us and may affect generations to come. Sometimes the people that look the least like us can astound us with their stories. When people open their hearts and speak of their fears and joys they touch our hearts because if we can be totally honest with ourselves we have sometimes felt the same or may do in the future.

So let us broaden our horizons, a new form of globalization, human globalization in harmony with the rest of the planet. A recognition, that even the woman that hurt you last week may also be hurting; the man that ruined your life may feel as hopeless as you have felt. We all perform to the best of our capabilities. Some of us are sparrows, others are eagles. We are molded by our circumstances and our capacity to change. For those of us who are capable of change, we could make a difference by showing that first we are human and then we are from whichever culture or religion we are born into or choose.

We shape our future.

Childhood

Good morning
You know we used to get up real early, so early our
parents were still in bed. The sun streamed in
through the curtains. But we daren't open them
otherwise they would hear the metal on the curtain
rail and know we were up.
We lined up the rocking chairs against the wall.
Jumped up on them and rocked them back and forth
with all our might. And we raced. Sometimes the
legs getting caught in each other and almost
catapulting us off but mostly going forward at a slow
but exciting pace. They were our horses as we
galloped across the dining room, knocking chunks
off the furniture. Smoothering our giggles and joy as
we crossed the dining room in those great rocking
chairs.
When we tired of this game if no one upstairs had
stirred we would make our way out into the back
garden, the fresh moist air catching our breaths, the
dew soaking our shoes. We hung upside down on
the bars of the swing or the apple tree. On the swing,
we swung so high that we thought we would fly to
sit on the clouds or swing around the top bar, loop
the loop. And when the chain chunked so hard we
jumped, airborn for those few seconds before we hit
the wet grass, saturated and happy.

Touched

He told me it was our secret. I need not tell my parents. We were small. Not long out of nappies, starting school. He touched me where nobody else did. I couldn't figure it all out.

He protected me from everyone like I was his little princess. No one was allowed to be as close to me as he was. He kept everyone away with his jealousy. Days mingled into months and years and still he was there. How can I write how I felt? I was so young. I only know how I feel now. Betrayed and hurt. Sad and damaged.

We are both married now and I have children. Nobody knows the extent of my hurt. Nobody knows how much sadness he has caused. He is still the strong figure in our family. He has his own successful life. Under the carpet crawl thousands of memories catching me off guard when I least expect it.

Will I ever heal?

Sandwiched

It is the very early morning. The weak sunshine is sneaking in through the cracks in the curtains. I sneak out of my bed and into my parent's bed. The heat there is nothing like it anywhere. Their big soft bodies in the morning. I snuggle in trying to make a space under her chin and sticking my bottom into the gap where her tummy is. I love it in here in the early mornings. The gentle snores of my dad. The heavy breathing of my mother as she stirs to pat my head. They are so used to me now. They never complain or shove me out. I drift off into a deep contented sleep. Knowing they are there and I am safe in their haven.

Slowly my eyes waken to the brightness. And I realise I am alone in the bed. How did they manage to escape? They left me here alone. It is not the same without them. Rubbing my eyes with my knuckles I wander half asleep to the bathroom and hear their voices downstairs.

Why didn't you wake me I whinged and my mam cuddled me and said she couldn't bear to stir my sleepy body. She knew I needed the rest.

Left

They have gone off and left me here. Here with my relatives who don't really want me, another mouth to feed, another head to look out for. Even my cousins are not that pushed about having me around. The numbers just aren't right for playing the game. I will have to wait till the next round and then somehow or other they forget and I am left standing there for hours on end just watching and wishing.

There is no point in crying. They tell me to stop whinging and be glad that I have a roof over my head. I don't care about a roof over my head. I want my mother. I want my dad too but I haven't seen him for so long I can hardly remember what his face looks like. I carry their photo all creased and battered in my pocket every day hoping that someday they will appear round the corner and I can run into their arms and they will carry me away from here. Here where I don't belong.

Dangling

I can hear them laughing and sneering. I wish the ground could swallow me up. They are so cool. They are the "in" gang. I don't belong. I am contented at home playing and minding my own business. But I can't go out of their way here. I am glad when I make it into the classroom without meeting them. I run the whole way leaving late so they will be gone on ahead. Breaktime is the worst. My arms feel like they are dangling down and my mouth moves all funny when I go to talk. No matter what I do they will always find something to laugh about. My hair, my shoes, the way I move, the way I talk, on and on it goes. On and on they get at me and each day seems like an eternity till I can get home within my own four walls and play with my dolls.

Sofa comfort

The music had begun. I always recognised it. My Dad had promised to look with me. The rest of the gang were out playing somewhere. It was actually glorious weather and here we were tucked up on the sofa looking at the telly. My Dad knew how much I loved these films. Maybe secretly he loved them too. It certainly felt like it. I had him all to myself.

The story was nearly always a bit tragic but she was such a survivor. Such a great little dancer. She danced through her life. Tapping all her worries into the floor. Tapping her way down those stairs of all those strange houses she stayed in. I admired that little curly head. She made me laugh. She made me cry. My dad would cuddle me closer as he felt my body shake from the sadness of it all. This little girl on the screen went through so much and I was going through it with her on those special afternoons with my Dad all safe and warm wrapped up in love on the sofa.

Easy life

Me and my sister share a bedroom. What fun we have. The sun streams in the cracks in the curtains and we are awake. Not knowing what time it is we lift the curtain looking out to see if there are any clues. But we don't look onto the street from here so all looks the same as the evening before. The garden blooming, new buds bursting through the old branches on the trees. Daffodils dancing in the wind. We cuddle back down under the covers. The sun might be shining out there but there is still a nip in the air in here. My sister has popped out to the toilet when she comes back in she sneaks into the bed beside me. Putting her freezing toes against the back of my calves. I stifle a yell, clouting her with the pillow. She grabs her pillow and we whack around a bit till we tire out and flop back down on the bed. Arms aching from whacking with the pillow.

She lifts up my nightie and talks into my tummy. Making me laugh as it tickles me. She screams into my tummy and it sounds all weird and mad. I pounce on her and tickle her till she's gasping. When she has recovered, she starts telling me about what they were up to in the garden yesterday, when I was up at my friends. Turns out a whole gang of kids were over, all pulling the pea-like things off the big green trees at the bottom of our garden. There was a massive war, boys against girls firing those peas and lashing the backs of legs with the long grass from our neighbour's garden. Must have been mad with all the crowd around. I wished I had been there. But then again it sounded just a bit too wild and I don't like getting hurt. My sister is a bit more of a tom boy. The wilder the better. She was glowing even telling the story. Our tummies started to grumble so we headed down to the kitchen to get some cereal. Saturday mornings and holidays are the best. We have the place to ourselves. At least for a little while.

Replaced

They only have eyes for her. My little sister. She is the apple of their eye now. I must admit she does look cute all wrapped up in his soft blue blanket. I could love her I know. It would be so easy. But she gets all the attention. I open my mouth. I want to tell them what happened in school. School is all new to me. Surely they want to hear my stories. But no, I have to be quite. They just have to change her or wash her or they just have to pop out to the shops. Everything is faster now. Faster and quieter and there isn't a minute in the day left for me.

My mother collapses down onto the sofa without my sister and I think great this is it. I can cuddle up to her like I always did. But she pushes me away. Gently, but very definitely. She says sorry but she is exhausted and sore. The breast feeding is getting to her, the sleepless nights. Nobody has any patience any more. Everybody is tired and cranky. I think when my Dad gets home it will be great. He will have time for me. But he says he has to help out my mam. I slam the door to my room. Put on my cassette loud. Trying to block them out. But there is a knock on the door. I have to turn it down. Good night. Sleep tight. Maybe I will have a chance tomorrow.

Looking great
These are my clothes. I stand here and look in the
mirror and sigh. I will never fit in looking like this.
No jeans like the rest of them. No just these brown
trousers. No nice cool shirts and T-shirts but these
horrible shirts beige, soft and musty looking. They
make me look how I feel; shoddy, misfit not smart
and cool. I have tried cutting off the long collar of
my shirt only to get a good talking to when I came
home about wasting good cloth and making a show
of the family. Don't they know I am making a show
of the family the way they dress me. I don't have
any choices. I don't know where my mother gets
these clothes but they are awful. I should be grateful.
My brother gets my hand downs and looks even
scruffier but somehow that scruffiness doesn't make
him look as odd as me all starched and dull with my
hair stretched over my forehead. The minute I am
out the door I bush it out a bit but it doesn't make
much of a difference. The girls will never look at me
like this. The fellas don't really want to be seen with
me. All such surface people you could think but
would you blame them? They don't want to be put
in the same boat as me.

Furry friend

She ran out bubbling all frisky and happy every time
I came to the door. I would nearly fall over with the
power of her. The wrestle in the hallway. Her
yowling and me squeeling. No human would ever
welcome you in this way. I loved her, my border
collie. She knew when I was sad too and she would
lick me and nestle into my legs and I dragged my
school bag through the hall door after a tough day.
We used to walk for miles in the forest her sniffing
and dancing around the place. The enthusiasm for
life bursting through her. She loved those walks and
I did too. It took me out of myself. The raw breeze
ripping around me, her racing off into the bushes
and coming back with a stick for me to throw for
her.
She had got slower the last few years. Sometimes
she brought back a different stick. The last few
weeks we hadn't been able to make it to the forest.
My faithful pal. She was suffering. We had brought
her to the vet so many times. Nothing was going to
make her better. Old age, nothing to be done.
She was put down this morning. I held her till the
last moment. Her eyes pleading with me. She knew
what was happening. It broke my heart, wrenched it
out seeing her there so helpless.
I carried her home, nearly collapsing with the weight
of her. My mam held open the door of the car. I just
sobbed and sobbed.
We buried her in the garden. My dad helped me dig
the hole for her. I couldn't do it in the end. I just

couldn't put her into the deep black hole. I rushed inside and up to my room. I just wanted to be alone. I left my parents in the garden nodding.
I went out when it was dark sat down on the wet grass and talked to her. Knowing she was listening. Knowing that she understood me. I missed her so much. I needed her now more than ever before.

Voyeur

I watch them play. I sit here on the edge of the playground. I know that they see me but somehow they just accept that I will always be there. I just belong at the edge. Watching and wondering how it would feel to join in. I don't want to take the first step. I don't want my mother to organise it. I just want to watch. Sometimes I nearly jump up in excitement and say something. Sometimes I even venture over to the sand pit and sit in it when nobody is there. If one or two kids come it is alright but not when the big gang comes. They all know each other. They fight and roar orders at each other. I don't like the noise. It is too much for me. I move off. They are just glad of more space. They are too busy in their own world. And somehow I think I am just as happy in mine. I wish my mother didn't always ask. "Did you play with someone"? "Do I want to call for someone?" It is ok if she asks. "Did you have fun?" I did in my own way. A bit envious sometimes, but not too unhappy.

Buddy

He asked me today if I wanted to play football. I had
been hanging around kicking my ball at the side of
the pitch. Yeah, sure! I answered cautiously. He
looked alright. He smiled showing the gap in his
teeth. Great! I passed him the ball. At first we just
past it back and forth but then he started to tackle
me. Automatically, I dodged him and made my way
to the goal hitting it into the back of the net.
A whole gang of lads approached the field. Shit,
now he will disappear off with them. But no it's ok.
I can be on his team. We are playing 5 a side and I
have the ball. We played for hours. It was dark when
I was heading home. God, I was a mess. I hoped my
mam wouldn't be mad. Mud everywhere. And I
have quite a bruise on my cheek when I got in the
way of a hard fast ball. God had that hurt. I had to
bite the inside of my cheek to stop the tears, my
bottom lip trembling. But they were nice, those
fellas. They didn't laugh and even looked concerned
asking if I was alright. I can go back out tomorrow. I
can't wait.

Operation

There was a lump where it shouldn't be. They had explained it all to me but I really didn't get it. It was kind of exciting going into hospital. None of my pals had been. But I was scared. I knew I didn't like needles or swallowing tablets. My mother assured me I would be alright.

We had to leave very early in the morning. I wasn't allowed to eat anything, not even a drop of water. I should have known that was strange. My mother would never let me out of the house in the morning without something in my tummy and here we were leaving with nothing to settle that queasy feeling. To tell you the truth I was so tired I could hardly get my legs to move. My mother dressed me gently. She was as uptight as I was. Her cheeriness was only skin deep.

We made our way down the road to the bus. I was amazed to see there were people on it. It seemed like the middle of the night. Where could they be going? My mother explained about all the things I never thought about; the people baking the bread, the people in the hospitals, the people looking after the electricity, etc. etc. Then I didn't feel so tired hearing about all these things that needed to be done. The bus ride felt like an eternity. When will we be there, I kept asking my mam. Soon, Soon. She repeated.

And soon was too soon. We went in the lift up to the right floor. I don't think my mother knew exactly where we were going. She hesitated a lot. It was very quiet in the hospital. Everybody must have been asleep.

A nurse came along and talked a lot to my mother. Then I was taken to a little room where I got a syrup. They said I should feel sleepy. But I didn't. My mother looked worried. The nurse explained that not all children react the same. How could I be sleepy when I wanted to know what was going on? Now I was in a wheel chair as they brought me in the lift. We arrived in a strange room. I had to climb up onto a trolley bed. Now I was scared. My mother wasn't allowed to come with me. Why not? She was always with me when things got tough. Why not now? It is not fair. I want her there. She seemed small as she waved as I disappeared around the corner. Now what?…..

I woke up screaming. How could anybody cut me? I am really angry. They cut me there and I didn't get to stop them…

I woke up and my mother looked at me smiling. I felt all drowsy. What had happened? I was hungry. I got something to eat. It is so nice that I can have biscuits. I have to eat slowly. They are all so nice to me. I felt stiff a bit sore. I didn't know where the pain was coming from. It was ok. The pain wasn't too bad. I wanted to go to the toilet. I had to go in a funny shaped tray in the bed……

Choice

They never asked me if I wanted to go with them.
They had visited regularly. But I belonged here with
my grandmother. I love her so much. She is here
with me everyday. She puts a plaster on my knee
when I fall. She hugs me good night. She tells me
stories and makes me laugh. She lets me help her in
the kitchen. I know she loves me too.

My heart is breaking as I wave her goodbye. I don't
want to go to that other place that I have only once
visited. I have a sister now it seems. But it is all very
strained. They all tell me I should be happy. I am
going to be in a lovely place with my parents and
sister. But I want to be here. Here where I know and
love.

I am angry. So, so angry. I cannot fight them. I am a
little girl who nobody is listening to.

Freshness

As my body hits the refreshing water and I dive to the bottom I know it is summer, my favourite time. I feel like a wet seal. My hair stuck to the side of my head, my skin silky with the water. Wow, what a feeling. The heat of the day dries me out after I swim to my favourite rock. I sizzle in the sunshine. My friend edges his way up on the rock beside me. We bask for a while in the sunshine before we dive again. I feel so part of this lake, the fish, the rocks, the moss. I have grown up with it. Tottering in as a baby, feeling the shock of the cold water, now loving it as I stretch and twist and wallow in my haven.

We hang out after, sitting on the short grass, laughing and carrying on with friends. We spend the summer here. Others have gone off to exotic places but for us this is our heavenly summer when the sun shines.

Pitch fever

It was raining finely. That drizzle that soaks your very bones. But I didn't care. I was enthusiastic as ever to get out onto the pitch, get my coat and trousers off. Get into the excitement of it all. I shook a bit with the cold and the jelly feeling in my legs and my tummy. I waved to them all on the side line. They have stood there in all weathers supporting me. Usually they are not all there at the same time but today is our big day. We are at the top of our league and this is our chance to win. We have never got this far before.

Some of the others straggled out onto the pitch. You wouldn't think to look at them that we had ever won a match. But it is just the early morning. Once we get going you should see them go. Scraggly Johnny suddenly will break into new life. I think he saves his energy the rest of the time being cool. Real cool. We line up all in our positions and that minute before the whistle goes is always so tense but today even more so. And we are off. Gerry passes the ball to me and I get it dribble along the middle and pass it over to Matt who slides past it. The ground is so slippy. Our opponents grab their chance and hare up the field but I am in there tackling them and I get it and pass it off to our side man. Up he sprints and before we know it he has shot the ball into the back of the net. I can hardly believe it. Wow, fantastic. We are off to a good start.

And so the ball goes back and forth. It is a tough match. I have made a complete idiot of myself a few

times. The ground being so slippy I have even fell out on my face after tripping over the ball. But the others aren't much better. And we are in the lead. We just have to beat them. We can do it. We are all awake now only another 5 minutes to go. I take my chance the field is open and run as fast as I can before all the defence get into place. Just as I feel his breath on my neck I shoot and it gets there. Somehow or other it makes its way into the corner of the net. Yes. Another goal for us. If we can ward them off now and even manage to get another goal we will have won the championship. Stay cool. We are not there yet. Never relax till the final whistle. What did I tell you? There they are, they have the ball again. Matt is in on them, he passes me the ball. They are all on me now. I just manage to get the ball away from me but Gerry isn't fast enough to get it. Our opponents have the ball and it looks like a sure goal for them and then it will be a draw. But no he has slipped just as he struck the ball and the ball slips off side. Corner!
We have to get this. We can't afford not to win now. And Matt gets the ball. Tearing down the pitch at an almighty speed. He is stopped in his tracks as the final whistle blows. We have made it. We are the champions today. Close call, but just what we needed, that single goal that made the difference. I shot it. Yes, Yes, Yeeess!
I loved the smell of the popping corn. I knew we would have a great day. I had asked all my pals from around the road. They were all coming. My mam

had rows of fairy cakes with icing all set out on plates. Big bowls of popcorn. Glasses for the lemonade.

Birthday girl

The day was fine. We could even go out in the garden.

We played blind man's buff but the fellas kept pulling the girls hair when they were blindfolded so my mother had to put a stop to that before it got totally out of hand. We swung out of the apple tree, we played pass the parcel. Then we gorged ourselves on all the goodies my mother had made.

I had got so many things for my birthday. I ripped open the packages as soon as I got them. The kids giving the presents often looking yearningly at them half hoping I wouldn't like them so that they could have them back. But I loved everything, the skipping rope, the toy watch in the coloured straw box, the magic colouring book where you just had to paint with water and the colours appeared.

Most of all I loved dressing up for my party. I always had a lovely frock on. My mam tied up my hair or put a slide in. I loved all the calling at the door. Knowing each of the calls was for me. The crowd in the dining room all swimming round in their new clothes looking all spruced up. My mother putting on the music for musical chairs always got the atmosphere going. The fellas making faces as they pretend danced around. The girls dancing around like fairies in their party frocks. We never had enough chairs so it was just the last one to hit the ground was out. We played enough rounds of it till we were sick of it and wanted something else. I never remember people going home. I must have been exhausted by then. They obviously drifted off as their mothers called for them. We all absently waving bye till only me and my sister remained with squashed popcorn on the floor. Our ribbons half hanging off our heads and the place in a general mess. Now I could really look at my presents.

Gasp

I sit upright in my bed, gasping trying to catch my breath. No hope. I can't get any air. Panic. No calm down. Get my inhaler. It takes a while before it starts to kick in and I so glad it is just beside me. I am trying to calm my breath but I feel like the back wall of my lungs is stuck to the front and that someone has lodged a log in my throat. I can't do it. I am sick of it. It is so tiring. I just want to rest. The more stressed I get the worse it is. I can't have my mammy run into me now. I am big now. I have survived it so many times before just breath now strongly and evenly. It is nearly impossible. I have to get the coordination right otherwise the medication all ends up on my tongue and it tastes rotten. My head is spinning. I have to get it right. Puff the inhaler and breathe. I think I have got it now, at least some of it seems to have got down. I need to get it again. It is easier now. The hissing is going now and I sound a bit better. I am getting there. The fear begins to fade.

Departed

I am sitting here on my bed, moping as my mam would say. I can't help it. I am so miserable. She moved away. My best friend. We did everything together. We were in the same class since we were only chisellers. At first she used to just come to my birthday parties. Then as we got a little older, she would call round after she had done her homework. We would hang out. Watching people from the window. Scoffing all the food my Mam made. Then we would call for others and play chasing or go on our rollerblades. We always had something to do. As the years drifted on we hung out more and more together just the two of us. Off to the cinema when we were allowed, playing computer games, looking at magazines, exchanging stories from school.

Now what. Nothing, that's what. I knew she was going but it happened so fast. After years of everyday, now I will be lucky if I see her once every few months.

I am just so sad, so lonely, so bloody hopeless in myself sitting on this bed and wishing that I could turn back time.

Wow how you've grown

The fire was lit in the front room. We had cleaned
the place from top to bottom. My mother was up to
high dough with all the preparations. My Dad had
gone up to collect the visitors. We were all dressed
up looking absolutely delightful. Finger nails
gleaming, hair smelling like a dream. Ribbons put in
for the special occasion. Oh, we loved the
excitement. We couldn't start to play anything with
the expectation that any minute they would be here.
It always took an age for them to arrive. It would be
dark by then. The fire would have settled down and I
was allowed to put another briquette on to liven it up
again. I think my mam was glad of the delay. We
brought in the things she had prepared to the dining
room. A lot of the things for eating weren't really
our cup of tea. The fancy stuff in glass bowls for
starters smelled all vinegary and looked all slimy.
The eggs had rings of green round the middle and
stunk to high heaven. Somehow or other I don't
remember eating anything at that big fancy table. I
think we were glad to eat in the kitchen all normal
looking and smelling food. Lovely turkey and ham
and lashings of spuds.

Then we heard the key in the door. We were out like
a shot. They nearly tripped over us. All swooning
down on us with "hasn't she grown". We were
proud of ourselves, standing there looking all smart
and collecting up the compliments like sponges. We
didn't mind the hugs and the kisses. We loved the
smell of perfume and a rub off my auntie's fur coat.

We would nestle into it later when they were all chatting in the sitting room. The place was full of chatter and laughter. It was just lovely. They all settled down into their seats. After the initial awkward chit chat the stories began. They probably didn't notice our ears grow bigger as we sat on the floor and took it all in. My Grandfather was great for the stories. He was outrageous in every possible way. They egged him on. The more he drank the better the stories got and he would tell a riddle to get us thinking.

After the dinner they would all return back in and my dad would get out the old tape recorder. We all had our go. Singing and telling stories, all competing to outdo the other. The atmosphere was great, warm and cosy, everybody grinning and everybody really happy.

Freedom
I had a list so long. I don't know how I was
supposed to fit everything into one rucksack let
alone try to lift it off the ground and carry it. I don't
think so. We had been talking about this trip since
last year. Some were afraid. Not liking the idea of
sleeping away from home. It never bothered me. I
had slept in friends and relatives houses without
mam and dad since I was young. The only thing I
was worried about was carrying my bag. I am not a
small girl anymore but this means my clothes and
boots are not small either and it is a big load. Mam
says she will come to the train station with me so I
know she will carry it, well I hope she does but after.
I can't quite imagine how we will manage.
But we are off now. We practiced cooking in our
cook group last week and it wasn't too bad we could
eat it. Curry is a great thing covers up a multitude of
tastes.
My Mam and Dad and little sister look more
tentative than I feel. I am rearing to go. I know we
have a great group in our room. Should be great gas.
Farewells out of the way we are on the train. Acting
the eejit having so much fun. Trying on each other's
cool hats and sunglasses.
We have a great class. 11 years old and what a sense
of freedom. We didn't get a minute to be lonely to
miss our parents or home. I think even the most
hesitant among us found the same. Well everybody
seemed to be joining in the fun. I must say I could of
cried when we went on that long hike. My feet and

legs were killing me. I thought I would never move my legs again. But that night we were still leaping from one bed to another laughing and squealing till the teachers came in pretending to be all serious. And by the way we didn't end up carrying our bags too far. Just off the train and a little bit up the road. Just to let us suffer a bit. Then a friend of our teachers came along in a van and hauled all the heavy rucksacks into the back and we felt we were walking on air.

Wow I can't wait for our next class trip. The food was ok but the fun just all being together day and night laughing till our bellies hurt compensated for any strange tastes at meal time.

And we're off
The cases were full of goodies. We always brought
so many presents and returned with many as well. It
was exciting the time leading up to going. Do you
think Granny would like this? But what about
Grandda he will feel left out. Have you anything for
him?
Usually we only went once a year. So though we
were on the phone regularly and I could feel their
closeness in my heart, it was just great to see them
really. The welcome was always great, the hugs, the
knowing we were special. They were special too.
The way they talked. The carry on. Something so
familiar about them. Something comfortable.
At long last we were heading to the airport. It was
great to get rid of our cases. Then we were free to
roam the airport. I am old enough now to buy a
magazine for the plane. But I know I probably won't
get to read it.
I love flying. I love the speed along the runway
before we lift off. And then we are up in the air and I
can look at the houses becoming like dolls houses
and the pattern of the fields stretching out belong
like a quilt on a huge bed. The squiggly lines of the
rivers. The snow-capped mountains in winter.
Yahoo. We are up. They are bringing along the
drinks. When I was small they even gave me some
little thing to play with.
Everybody is in great humour until we start to
descend and then it's yawning and blowing and
puffing trying to unblock our ears. This is the bit I

hate and I always forget until it is happening. Pop. I managed to get my hearing back and get that searing feeling out of my head.

But my sister is struggling nearly crying now and my mother is trying to urge her to yawn or blow her nose. The chewing gum really doesn't help but we chew like mad anyway.

We have landed blocked ears and all. There is a scramble for the bags but we wait on, till the rush is over and head out. The cold wind catches our breath when we get to the door. That wind would knock the cobwebs off you. We have arrived and I am glowing, my stomach leaping all over the place. We get to the exit after we get our bags and there they are. As they always are. Ready to grab us and squeeze us tight. A big bears hug. We hug back with all our might. The start of a really nice holiday.

Dejected

I don't know why I was born. Why did they bother
with the effort. They don't care about me a bit. My
younger brother is the darling of the family. He
charms them with his wit and humour. I only take
my fathers anger. The leather belt hitting me,
stinging my skin. I would go, disappear but where
would I go. They wouldn't miss me. But they would
find me drag me back to begin the cycles of fear,
desperation, hate and relief.
I shouldn't hate them, they are my family. They are
all I have in this world. I have friends but I know
that they come and go too and can't be trusted. I just
feel so alone. Nobody is special to me. Nobody
treats me like I am their darling.
I just want someone to notice. I am here too. I need
someone to really see me, hug me, comfort me and
make me feel that it I am alright as I am.
I am good in school. I do my best. I study hard and
get the results they want. I am waiting for their
praise for their approval. But it is never enough.
There are always more demands. Pushing and
pushing for perfection. Everything is tight in me. I
am lean and hard. Sprung tight. Someday I will let
loose. Someday when I have my own life, I will
build my own life, a life better than this and let them
know what I really feel. I will not always be
dependent on them. What never really leaves me is
their disapproving voices in my head.

Way home
We mooched along. Hopping up the steps and down.
Collecting bits of flowers and nice pebbles. My pal
collected me at the same time every day. We were
lost in our own world chatting and singing.
Watching squirrels disappear into the trees as we
came round the corner. Each season had its
specialities. Looking for the shiniest chestnuts in
October, collecting the loveliest flowers in May.
Splashing in the deepest puddles in March. Rolling
down the freshly cut grass on small hills in July.
Watching passersby watching their wierdness or
their coolness. Wishing our lives away. Dreaming of
great castles and clothes. Petting stray cats and dogs.
Letting them cuddle into us. The cats pressing their
warm bodies against our legs as we continued on our
way. Day in, day out for years and years in
wellingtons, sandles, muddy boots, teeshirts, hot
jackets, wooly hats. The path was worn by us with
our big school bags. Generation after generation
walking to the school house that smells of school.
It had been warm and sunny for so long, we had
made our mud pies in the garden decorating them
with sprinkled daisy leaves. We had played horse
show, taking out all the stuff as we could manage
from the shed, spacing them around the garden. We
had such a laugh, galloping round and round trying
to make the jumps higher and higher, screaming
with excitement and terror.
We had skipped on the road, everyone joining in
singing and dancing over the rope till the sun went

down. We had burst bubbles of tar with our toes. And now it was time for our show. It had taken an age to deliver all the slips of paper into the neighbourhood letter boxes running for our lives when dogs came barking and yapping at our heels. We had practised our dancing. Practised our play, done our balancing act so many times without falling into the coal bucket. And now the side gate was open. The apple tree was in full bloom. The grass nicely cut and we were giggling our heads off. Hardly able to stand straight with the excitement. My mother had concerns of her own. She was busy baking, to give the kids something for their money, just incase they didn't like our show - I only found that out recently. Anyway, there they were all lined up on the grass in front of us. Days of practising behind us. We did all our bits. And it was all over in a flash. So much expectation on their faces and this was it. Was this all that we had produced? It seemed that we had so much more material. But things speed up when you are nervous and we were glad that they were all happily munching on my mothers goodies. We gathered up the pennies and headed to the shop and down the park with bags of sweets and popcorn. Thrilled at our hard earned money.

Safe

She held my hand and I grinned feeling happy in my whole body. Warm and safe as we made our way along the country lanes. The sun was shining. My sandles which had dug into me at the beginning of the summer now felt soft and comfortable. I didn't mind the walk. She chatted about the old times. She was lost in a world of her own but acknowledged my smile as she looked down to me from time to time. I loved to hear her voice. I loved to hear those stories I had heard many times before.

The brambles climbed up the side of the road and I could see the berries. Black as could be. Bursting with juice, waiting for me to grab them.

Once again I forgot the thorns at my legs. They were protecting their fruit, keeping me at bay. I could only get those low down. The big juicy ones my mother gathered in the plastic bag. The ones I got went straight into my mouth. I always checked for the worms as my mother had taught me.

As we moved along the hedgegrow the bag got fuller and I was quite a mess. A new pattern on my dress, nice purple splotches. My mother wasn't so impressed but her mood didn't change. Now that I was stuffed with berries what I looked forward to most was smelling the berries cooking in the oven with the sponge on top. The purple colours seeping up the side. The first bite of sweetness meeting sourness. The end of summer taste.

Helpless
They were fighting again. It started out quite harmless but we knew it was escalating when he slammed his fist on the table. If only it would stop there. The others ran away but I wouldn't, I watched from behind the sofa. He hit her. My mother, who tucks me into bed at night and cooks the finest of things to fill my tummy. She was hurt. I heard her small cry. He can't do that. That's not right.
I will stop him. I will tell him it's not right. I am not afraid.
But, as I appeared in the kitchen she screamed "Get out, Get out of here. Why is she mad with me, I just want to help.
I run and cry and hide so no one can see my tears.

Roaming free till tea

We rushed in, dumped our school bags, kissed our mam and off out we hared as quick as we could hearing her voice echo in the background. "Do you have much homework?"

School was behind us. We wanted out. Swinging out of the old tree, robbing apples, hanging out down by the river. Letting tiny insects tickle our arms and screaming as monster insect heads appear out of the mud as we clean out the dirt around the shores with ice cream sticks. Do you know the taste of grit and dirt? The black chewing gum we scraped off the paths. Who ever would have thought that I would like this sticky dirty mess and still squeel if my mam missed a lump in the mashed potatoes?

Sick of it

It was just a never ending story. From the moment he got home from work. They picked and prodded at each other or ignored each other or started roaring. I never knew which was worse the silence and tension like a storm building up or the fear shaking in my inner core when they started roaring. They never hit each other so I suppose that was something to be grateful for but they never laughed and carried on like I had seen other parents. Normal conversations with normal themes were not really so common. Always who was to blame for what? Always afraid to take sides but been given a side by their reference to our similarity with the other parent. Oh she is so like you in that way…..

Collected from school early

We stayed with my big brother in the nearest town. The secondary school was there. I really liked going to school. I loved all the languages. We had so much fun but I missed home.

My father came every week at the same time to take us home for the weekend.

We really looked forward to hearing him coming in the door downstairs.

Today my brother came and said we were going home. I didn't know what he was talking about. This wasn't the day. My father always comes.

Why are we going now?

Nobody answered my questions. We had to hurry to catch the bus.

When we got to the gate of our house I knew something was up. So many cars. Where was my mother? I screamed looking for her. She was often sick and I thought that maybe something was wrong with her. I was uncontrollable in my grief. Where is she?

Everybody was trying to hold onto me to explain but I couldn't hear them.

Slowly the words sunk in. My mother was fine. My father was dead.

We had only sat together a few days before. How can that be? He was fine. He was strong. He was my father who loved me and took care of me so much.

His heart had stopped and now he is gone.

Leaving for the mountains
We had packed everything. It was early morning and
as the weak sunlight seeped in the window we
folded our mattresses and made our way out into the
morning air. It was fresher than we had felt in a
while. The scorching heat of the day was a few
hours off. We had to make our way as far up the
mountain as possible.
The animals were all ready. Our parents had been up
before us getting everything ready.
We loved the adventure. We did this every year but I
never tired of it.
We would be walking for a few days. We didn't
rush. My father set the pace making sure everyone
was ok. When I had been young I would be tied onto
my mothers back as she rode the horse slowly up the
mountain.
We stopped in the villages along the way. Bought
what we needed and carried on unless it was too hot.
I loved when we pitched the tents and when we did
our chores we could disappear off until sunset
playing and singing in the vast expanse of
countryside around us. We never seemed too tired to
play.
We milked the sheep, made cheese and sold it to the
villagers. Everyone seemed relaxed and happy. It
was hot in the afternoons and we were lazy in the
heat but happy for the fresher air of the mountains.

Exposed

She is such a bitch. I just cannot believe that she would do such a thing. We have been friends for as long as I can remember. I trusted her. We confided about everything. Why did she have to tell?

It all started several months before. I had a relationship with the hottest fella you have ever set your eyes on. I was swept away. He was so charming. I couldn't keep my eyes off him. I was so thrilled when we started going out. I know it must have been hard for my pal as we didn't meet up as much as before. I just wanted to give my new relationship a chance.

When we met I told her everything. Really everything. How we giggled those afternoons away. It was all so new to both of us. She had had a boyfriend the previous summer and had been equally excited though it had ended fairly suddenly when her father found out he had been drinking when they had been out together and he brought her back late. Lots of crying and shouting and at least one big broken heart. They only nodded at each other now when they met. Both too embarrassed to talk about the whole scene.

But this is all beside the point. I had comforted her in her hour of need as friends should and so it was only normal that I would tell her when my relationship with my boyfriend progressed and we slept together for the first time. He wasn't any less nervous than I was. We really were like kids but excited terrified, thrilled kids and though it had felt

great up until that it wasn't like I thought it would
be. It was sore and not comfortable and I didn't feel
as excited anymore and I know he could feel my
hesitation too. All a bit of a mess. A real mess
actually.
I shouldn't have told her. But of course it was the
only thing on my mind. I was sure she would notice
something had changed about me. I mean I felt so
different myself. I just wanted to let her know that
she didnt need to hurry. It wasn't all it was cracked
up to be. It was much nicer just kissing and feeling.
That's what I felt. But because she hadn't had this
experience she looked at me. Concerned but also a
bit strange. I don't know what was going on in her
head.
I made her promise not to tell anyone. I didn't really
even feel I needed to mention that but you never
know.
Well a few weeks later my boyfriend was really
strange with me. Cold and hurt. I couldn't make him
out. I knew he wanted to talk but dreaded what he
wanted to say. It couldn't be good judging by the
expression on his face. I was mortified when he told
me. The ground could of opened up and I would
have been glad. He was raging. He had heard fellas
in college talking about us. Sniggering saying we
were a joke of a couple. That I couldn't get it in.
horrible things like that. Oh God. Oh no. She had
told someone. No, I had told her but had made her
promise. Shit, shit, shit. I wanted to strangle her. I
wanted to do the same to myself. I just stood there

frozen to the spot when he questioned me about it. Guilt written all over my scarlet body. I said nothing. Nothing would change things. I had trusted her. I had needed to share my confusion and now I was left with nothing. My boyfriend looked at me with disdain. How could I blame him? When he left the room the silence just exploded in my ears. I felt a stone drop in my heart and I felt so alone. It's not really the thing you go running to mammy and daddy to tell. It is your best friend you turn to. But never again. Never again.

Cake
We didn't need much to make those cakes. A bit of
margarine, sugar, eggs and flour and some fruit.
Anything to make it juicy.
We left the margarine out all morning hoping it
would soften. The caravan was heating up with all of
us cooped up in there all day. The rain. pelting down
outside, drumming on the roof. The racket it was
making made it difficult to hear each other
sometimes. The condensation ran down the
windows. Wow, are we a hot family?!
We had played draughts and cards all morning.
Sometimes the odd screaming session as one felt
hard done by or was sick of losing. Then we were
getting bored, sick of the same games. No let up on
the rain. So we started on the baking. It was always a
bit of a bother lighting that gas oven. We were all
terrified of it, even my mother. But she seemed to
get it going no bother today. I was always afraid it
will explode and we will all be blown to eternity.
It didn't take long to get the sponge mixture ready.
Each doing their bit. One beating the hell out of the
margarine and sugar. One cracking the eggs and
only dribbling a bit on the table and the last one
folding in the flour. Then we spread over the apples
or the rhubarb or the blackberries and we popped in
into the oven. My mouth is watering now even
remembering the smells coming from that oven. The
great thing about baking in a caravan as you are
nearly eating the cake before it is out of the oven. It
smells so gorgeous. And hot. Hot as a sauna it was.

No wonder we often didn't know the windows were leaking from the rain till it was too late and the mattresses were soggy. The steam from the heat in that caravan was pouring down the window and as we waited for the cakes to bake we drew funny faces with our fingers and watched the spiders gather up their prey in their carefully spun nets.
The first bite, steaming hot, that moist spongy mass cannot be described in words.

Out of the way
Nobody can see the marks now. But when I was
smaller my body bore the bruises of my father's
anger. I cannot remember the first time. It all blurs
into one now. But certain times he was just wilder
than others and they stick in my mind. I wasn't the
only one but it just seemed to be me more often than
the others. I was caught easily. The others obviously
got the signal quicker and got out of his way. Others
can blame their father's drunkenness for all the
damage done to them. At least they could love their
fathers when they weren't drunk. But I never felt I
loved that man. He was like a volcano bubbling
constantly. He was ready to lash out for no reason.
He was so strict. We had to keep in line. We daren't
make a noise at the dinner table. We had to be on
guard in the house at all times. Hoping not to get in
his way. We tried to stay out of the house as much as
possible. But he had his rules to be abided by so we
dare not be late for evening prayers.
It hurt, it always did but I never knew if I was
weeping with the pain or the hopelessness of it all.
Knowing that no matter what I did, it would never
be good enough. As I took the beating I swore that
as soon as I had enough money I would leave this
house and never return. But it hasn't turned out like
that. My mother, my dear weak mother; she who
never said a word against him; who was as fearful as
the rest of us. I did not want to desert her. So
although I live away from home I always return to
visit. He is quieter now he still has that iron look

about him but his fluid anger is expended or buried.
I don't trust him. He knows I hate him. I can't think
that anything will ever change that. But he is old
now and I do my duty helping them out mainly for
my mother's sake.

Playing cards
It is that time of the evening. The sun has gone
down, the birds have gone home to their nests. We
all gather round the table. All our worlds unite for
those few hours.
My father deals the cards. I watch in fascination as
he shuffles the cards with a speed that I imagine
would make those in the casino be jealous. I will
learn this too.
The concentration rises. We check the faces of the
others hoping for a clue of what they have in their
hands. A crooked grin of my brother when I know
he has the best card. The mischievous laugh of my
father as I size him up. He knows I am learning fast.
And the game begins. My hand is good but I have to
be fast. I have to get in there before the rest of them.
No, just as I had planned my next move my brother
puts down a card that upsets my whole strategy.
How does he always manage to do that? I am mad
but I don't let him know. There are other
exasperated sighs from around the table. I change
the situation again with my good card and it is my
last chance. Maybe I can win. But no my mother has
won again. She has it all sized up.
Maybe next round I will have a chance.

Growing up fast

There was a knock on the door. A policeman. Were the neighbours complaining about the noise we made last night? He looked very solemn. Not sure what he wants. Wish he would get started. He uttered my name. How does he know I live here? I am only here for the summer.

We don't have a phone. He was asked to contact me saying that I should go home. There had been an accident. My boyfriend had been involved. No further information.

I don't know what happened next but soon after that I was standing on the side of the road with my friend. We were hitching a lift home. Why we didn't ring home I don't know. It is hard to get a telephone box that is working. Why we didn't take the bus I am not sure either. Maybe we knew there wasn't one till the evening and just wanted to start as soon as we could. All I know is it was a long journey. We had hitched this stretch before. Usually one or two lifts and we would be home. But today everybody was just going a bit up the road. We took every lift and slowly we made our way home.

Maybe it was good the journey took so long. Maybe it gave me time to think. Why would they go to the bother of ringing the police on a Sunday morning? Why would they send out someone especially to our door if it wasn't serious?

I felt so strange in my body. Knowledge and denial mixing and churning me up inside. We tried to make

light of it. He was a trickster. He was probably ok
but just wanted me to be home.
Several hours later when we were totally exhausted,
when we couldn't lift ourselves to pretend we were
cheery anymore, we arrived at the hall door. We
only knocked once and my mother was there. I knew
by her face. I mirrored her face and felt all my
energy drain out of me.
She didn't say much. She didn't have to. He was
dead.

Getting school results
The anticipation is really getting to me. I cannot
stand it. I know I put my best in the last month but
will it be enough.
We have a great bunch in our class. We have such a
bloody laugh. You wouldn't believe the things my
pal comes out with. The faces she makes. It just
cracks me up. Then I realise I have missed that bit of
the lesson. It will take me an age to figure that out.
Maybe the others will know what the teacher has
been rabbiting on about. God, but she is so boring.
No, I can't imagine I will ever utter a word of
French from my lips once school is over. But as
French is one of the main subjects, and to put it
mildly it is not my strong point, I have to do
something.
I studied like mad the last few weeks, cramming it
all into that head of mine. I felt my head would burst
and all the pages would spill out of my ears. Funny
thing is, my head might have been full of French but
it was so crammed I couldn't sort all that
information out when I was shivering in myself
sitting in those exam halls. I tried to calm myself
down. Suddenly I really wanted to do well. I didn't
want to repeat this pain.
So I was so jumbled in myself. I am not sure what
sorts of results I will get. Even in the subjects that
are usually no problem to me.
This summer. My last long summer holiday. I
should be able to enjoy but the niggling at the back
of my head. Going through those questions now.

Knowing that I could write it now so much clearer. I just hope I pass. I don't need to show I am a genius just not a complete idiot.
Please let me pass.

Tingle

I didn't know him very well but I got so excited when he was around. I had seen him at the youth discos a few times. I was so embarrassed when he caught me looking at him. I went bright red. I could feel even my toes glowing in my boots.

He asked me to dance. I was sweating and trying to get some words out of my mouth so he wouldn't think I was a fool. Of course I would dance. Isn't this what I have been waiting for? The song finished and I thought he would drift off. No he stood there, his arm still around my shoulder. I had such a weird feeling in my body something between excited and sick. When he touched my hand again, it tingled. God I was melting here. I was relieved when the next song started. He started to dance again. I watched his mouth as he chatted. He watched mine too. And suddenly like two magnets our mouths were touching. Lips tingling. I was shocked and thrilled and didn't want it to stop but thought I should stop anyway. He smiled; we hugged and continued to dance. We laughed and swung around. I felt free. I had kissed a boy and it was nice. Really nice, 'cos I really liked him. I think by the twinkle in our eyes we have a lot more kissing to do.

Ow, that hurt.
My head smacked off the ground. I had been flying
along on my bicycle, downhill with the wind rushing
in my face. And now. I kept coming in and out of
the world. Who are those people around me? Out
again. It is raining. I thought the sun was shining.
"Come in out of the rain". Black again. I am sitting
up. What am I sitting on? They are bringing me
somewhere. I am walking towards a car. I am
talking. Do I know these people? Black again.
The hospital. The nurse. The questions. How stupid
do they think I am? I am 23. Amn't I.
I never know who the prime minister is. They keep
changing and they don't do anything dramatic. They
all fade into one big blob.
Then I am in the bed. No one is visiting me. Nobody
knows I am here, I realise.
They keep checking my eyes, the whole night
through. I wish they would leave me in peace. But
my hip. Why don't they check that? It is so hard to
walk. Every time I want to cough. I think my body
will explode with the pain. Sneezing is worse, it
catches you off guard.
The next day is actually worse. I can really feel the
pain. I just ache all over. I am so very tired. I wish
my mother was here to hug me. Somebody make me
feel better. News has got out that I am in the
hospital. Somebody from the factory saw me.
Sounds like I did a perfect somersault and am lucky
to be alive. There was so much traffic. The fact that I

didn't fall into the path of an oncoming car is a feat
to be proud of I guess.

Dinner for more than one

We had cleaned around the flat. We don't have much to clean up. We all have only lived here a year. We are all in our twenties working together. We have our differences. But get a load of food in and a few drinks and we have the best parties. We all chipped in some money and some of us started cooking earlier in the day. The others would be arriving later. We were making chilli con carne and garlic bread and cassata for afters.

I love the smell of fried onions. As they turn a golden brown and the smell wafts through her house, I long to get a load of mashed potatoes and mix it all up together and gobble the whole lot up. As I cut the peppers I try one and leave my images of spuds and onions behind me. In go the peppers till they are roasted nicely. And then the chillies. In goes the meat the garlic and the tomatoes and it is looking more like the real thing. My friend is studying catering and management. So she knows what to be doing. I have only baked at home a few times. So I am assistant to the chief today. It is such a laugh. We keep tasting the chilli at all stages but we keep sipping red wine as well. So we can't be too sure how everything is progressing. The garlic bread of course had to be sampled too and then I am afraid all our senses were dulled. The chilli didn't seem to be hot at all. A bit more chilli should do it. Saved by the bell, they all arrived in. They must have met in town.

Umm it smells divine. They were all storming the kitchen. No. paws off. We will be dishing it up in a minute. Can you bring in the plates, the knives and forks and can you open another bottle of wine? This one is nearly gone.

And the moment of truth as they all took their first mouthful. Silence and then screams and coughing. My god. What did you put into this? It burns the mouth off me. Wow, is this hot stuff. Sorry we tried it. Couldn't see, that it was hot at all. They looked at us grinning. Yeah sure. We didn't mention the wine or the garlic bread. Anyway they loved it in the end. Any excuse to drink more wine to dampen the hotness of the chilli. Any excuse to pat each other on the back as they coughed when they hit an unchopped chilli. We recounted our stories told a million times. We got merry as the night went on. Hanging out, laughing, lolling on each other, tickling and slagging each other. Simple delights of growing up with good food and good company.

Hit

My perception of life changed drastically this
evening as I made my way home from work. I heard
a screech of brakes and very loud thud and saw her
fly into the air. She must have landed on something
sharp perhaps the corner of the pavement as there
was blood everywhere. I couldn't stop shaking. I
was only just behind her. What made her run out
into the traffic at the last second? It was rush hour.
Bumper to bumper traffic in all directions. The car
had thought it would make it through the orange
light. Obviously it speeded up and she was
obviously in a hurry to catch that bus that was now
just pulling away from the stop. Everybody craning
their necks to see what had happened. It took a few
moments for a young lad to run across to the pub
and get them to ring for an ambulance. Cars that
were further back started to hoot their horns not
knowing what had happened.

Total mayhem. And what did I do. Absolutely
nothing. I stood there shaking glued to the spot. It
could have been me. I have taken quite a few
chances running across the road but it is more than
that. The skin holding everything together has been
burst. The body that moved so lightly before, who
knew what it wanted, now lies there in a terrible
mess. I am shattered knowing that it is a very thin
skin holding all those functions together. A split
second and the compact and wonderful body has
been changed. I stand there and try to recover, try to
be of help but others are busy functioning. I check

that I am not making any mistake in my shocked state. Wobbling I make my way over to the bus and like all the others waiting there just stand there just trying to take it all in.

The mountain beckons
Looking back now I try to think what motivated us
to get up on those dark grey mornings. We had been
out till all hours drinking and carrying on. The
drizzle was incessant and I knew my rainwear
wouldn't hold out the day. My boots were cheap and
I would have blisters for the week. But nothing
could stop me going.
We all met at the bus stop in town. All arriving from
all parts of the city.
We were all in college together. Some of us knew
each other well, others were new recruits.
The wooly hats, the mucky boots, the old trousers.
Fashion wasn't really a word you could use on this
bunch.
After an age, the bus arrived and off we hobbled.
Those boots really made us all waddle.
To tell you the truth I never noticed the weather too
much there was so much conversation. So much to
laugh about. We were bent up double some times
with stories of the antics of the night before. They
say drinking isn't good for your liver but maybe the
laughing that goes along with it and after helps to
conteract some of the effects.
The first bit on the road has us wrecked before we
had even started but once we got to the soft ground
of the mountain it was easier. Our rainwear sloshing
through the heather and gorse bushes. Somebody
racing, bit of bog in their hand aimed at the other.
Oh no, somebody is up to their ankles in bog water.
Off with the boots. Empty them out and wring out

those socks. Could do a good advertisement for washing powder with them. Before and after….
As we trundled on, the rain lashing at our faces now we were quieter each one in the own bit of misery, boots hurting a bit, the effects of the night before seeping into the body just as the rainwater seeped through the seams of our jackets.
Then it seemed like forever till we reached the top. How glad we were when it cleared a bit and we got to see what was around us but more often than not we found a hollow and nestled down in the heather hoping to keep our bottoms dry and chewed on the sandwiches or whatever we had stuffed in our bags at the last minute that morning.
The food in our stomachs gave us a boost. We got going before it got too cold and we were on our way again. Laughing and talking, slagging each other. Friendships made on those trips last till today. Now I don't venture out voluntarily in the lashings of rain unless to the shops.

Sing your heart out

We sat there bursting at the seams. We had been hungry all day but certainly made up for it this evening. My friend was a great cook. We had a few bottles of wine between us all and now the singing had begun.

It wasn't arranged. It never was. It was just part of coming to their house. The lads would get out the guitars and we would all sing. Sing usually the first verse of so many songs. The odd song we knew all the verses. Our heads lifted up. Often our eyes closed. Our voices joining and leaving each other's. We are warm in our hearts. Sometimes the words of the songs touching a chord with experiences from our own lives. Loneliness, broken hearts, new love. Many a tear was shed on those evenings. The effect of the wine, the warmth, the music stirring up the wells of our hearts. But we continued on to the next song. Rebel songs for causes long fought. Uplifting and throaty. All gusto, we often rose to our feet, laughing and carrying on.

We are no superstars, no one with a career in music. Just a group of pals singing their hearts out for all they are worth and hoping the neighbours wouldn't complain.

Bird's eye view

Sitting on the top of the building looking at the city
stretch out before me. I am far away from home. I
am independent. I am free to make any decision I
want to steer my life in the direction I want. When I
come down into the city nobody will notice that I am
here. But I feel my presence stronger in myself than
I have ever done before.

The weight of the rucksack on my back. Everything
I need in there, nothing more nothing less, no
cluttered room. I decide where I want to go, whether
I want to hang on another few days when the
weather is good and the company relaxing.

Looking at all the news bulletins before I headed off,
you would think there wasn´t a safe place left on
earth. You would think that people were only greedy
and mean and arrogant.

But I have met them all. The goodhearted and the
mean bastards. What amazed me are all the really
nice people. People who have nothing to gain by
helping me get my rucksack down from the top rack,
who give me change for the bus when the bus driver
tells me I can't use a note, people who help me find
my way, who let me wash my clothes in their friends
washing machine, who share their flat with me when
I miss my plane, who bring me to meet their parents
and feed me and treat me like royalty, who wave me
off as if I am their daughter.

It was worth travelling to see and feel all this. When
I think about it I realise I only had two bad
experiences nasty fellas who really shook me up

though I got away lightly. But all the others were so great and their warm hearts touched my heart and gave me hope for the future. Let me go home knowing that although the baddies hit the headlines, there are so many goodies just being nice right now.

Taken

They came out of nowhere. I had just left the public toilet. Trying to juggle all my bags and belongings. It had been so dirty in the toilets I couldn't manage everything in the cramped space.

Out of thin air literally they came and took everything. But then it wasn't enough. They wanted my money. My money belt and passport everything they ripped off. I must have been knocked unconscious. The pain seared through me. I just didn't expect it. I didn't put up a fight. It was all too much. Too fast I couldn't grasp what was going on. They had a big knife. It was on my throat and then all was black. They had ripped me apart. They weren't satisfied with just my belongings. They took everything of mine. Every tiny private part of me. I woke up weeping on the pavement. A terrible nightmare. Everything sore more than sore. I wanted to die.

I howled inside. Someone must have heard me. Someone took me away and I woke up in a warm bed. Really aching now, confused and hurt.

They fed me, dressed me, and looked after me so gently. Their concerned eyes. The warmth they showed me I will never forget just as I won't forget what went before. I could never tell my parents. They hadn't wanted me to go travelling alone. But so many people travel alone. I am not conspicuous. I didn't flaunt what I had. I never thought this could happen to me.

I have gone through some hell years since. Looking on, nobody would know the cause. I just couldn't get it together. I just don't feel good in myself. Hiding myself in big pullovers. Not looking for attention. Trying to excel in College and work but I can never be good enough.
Things are better now. But will never be quiet the same. How a few minutes can change your whole life and you can't even talk about it.

It could be me
I lie here freezing as the sun comes up weakly over
this vast city. In all these months I still haven't got
used to the cold. I cover myself with whatever I can
find. Old boxes newspaper anything but it is never
enough and this. It is supposed to be spring. I would
never last a winter. I can't believe it is me out on the
streets. I used to pass people like me and be a bit
afraid, embarrassed even a bit disgusted. I never
realised how slippy the slope is when you start to
slip off the main rail of life. It is very easy not to
have enough money to be able to pay your way, at
least in this big city where I know practically
nobody.
I got mugged.
That was the start of it. I have no insurance couldn't
get medical help. Then I couldn't show up for work
in the state I was in. I didn't have enough money for
the hostel and so things started to go downhill. I am
illegal here. I don't have a permit. So I can't go
claiming any benefits.
I am terrified out here on the streets at night
knowing I could be killed but I try to keep out in the
open so that I will be noticed. The dark alleys are so
dark and damp. I walk and walk the evenings till it
seems safe enough to lie down. I nod off. But as the
icy coldness of dawn gnaws at my ankles I wake and
try and bring myself to start another day.
I struggle to sit up, stretch jump up and down to get
the circulation going. I head towards the promenade.

Get a bit of heat into me in the suntrap there along
those tall white buildings.
I get rougher looking by the day and people look
like they are afraid of me. Don't they know I am like
them. I don't want this life. I didn't choose it. It
happened and it is very hard to get my old life back.
Nobody would give me a chance looking and
smelling like I do.

Recovering gently

We had been out dancing the night before. To tell you the truth I am not sure if it was the few drinks we had, the spinning round till all hours or just the lack of sleep but I feel like a dog's dinner and I look like one too.

I meet my friend coming out of the bathroom. Well that is a relief. She looks like I feel.

I head back into bed even though it must be coming up to midday and the sun is streaming through the window. The floor is freezing beneath my feet and it takes a while for my toes to warm up again. I take up the book from beside the bed. It is hard to focus on the page. I read a few pages before my fingers began to freeze and I tuck back down into the bed and doze off again for a little while. I hear the door slam below and think God I better get up. I ease my way out of the bed, hop into the shower and dress and hear the door slam again then my friend cheery call. So you're up then, are you, sleepy head? Look at the head on you.

I can't retort, same to you, as now she looks as fresh as a daisy.

She has the milk and fresh bread. God, she's a darling.

I make the tea. We divide up the Sunday paper. Get the hot buttered toast into us and head into the living room. It is cold despite the sunshine. This time I pop round to the local shop get a bit of coal to light the fire.

It's not long before I'm home again. It is always a
bit of an effort to get the fire going. We have the old
newspapers rolled up with the few sticks and the
coal on top. A few firelighters get the flames going.
Not that easy to get the draft right. But we have the
newspapers sealing the front of the fireplace and we
can feel the wind sucking at the fire now and we
know now we have it going. We lie back on the
couch exhausted, grabbing for more newspaper to
read.
As the light fades on this sunny winter day we
recount the antics of the night before.
Then the telly goes on and we are glued to it. Cosy
watching the flames of the fire, feet up, eyes half
closed. No effort at all. The only effort of today will
be to haul ourselves back into bed later so we can be
up for another week of work in the morning.

Yes, Yes Yes

I was very much in love. Terrified but excited at the whole thought of going to meet up with my boyfriend. I thought well if it doesn't work out I can get work picking fruit. I wouldn't be in a hurry to go home to admit the mistake that they were sure I had made.

We had met on a bus. He, the musician with the straw hat with just the rim. Me, the curly headed girl wandering the world excited but a bit lost.

He played his music and I followed him, my very own pied piper. I was n't thinking anything in particular, just fascinated by him. Viewing from afar. He was interesting and funny. A bit odd and yet so entertaining. He brought joy to the bus we were on. Within the first few days I couldn't take my eyes off him. I wanted to know what made him tick.

We walked together on and off in the group. We cooked together, travelled together but there were always other people around. Other people who seemed just as interested as I and that he seemed just as interested in.

After a game of pool where I had been his partner, he seemed to be interested in so many people, I thought I would head off to bed. I thought, once again I had fallen for a Romeo who wouldn't be interested in me and I was just going to cause myself upset and heartache.

Just as I reached the door of my cabin he caught up on me, tapped me on the shoulder and asked me if I would like to go for a walk.

I felt my heart jump. I was thrilled, scared but
happy. Of course I was eager to have him to myself.
I felt special. I have always hung out with male
friends but they see me as their sister and though
their love is really important to me I wanted
someone to want me especially.
So our relationship began. I felt as though I had
known him for a thousand years but at the same time
everything was new. The expressions on his face-
how to read them. His foreign accent, his loss for
words, his music, his bare feet, his mad laugh, the
way he made me feel when he was close. The
electricty of it all. The gathering thunder when he
was upset. The amazement at myself for feeling so
strongly. Strong enough to feel like a gypsy
intoxicated by his music. We could fight and hate
each other just as much as love each other. I had
never been able to do this with any one else.
On the 6 th day he gave me a key ring and said
jokingly when I grew into it he would marry me. So
it would be a while then, I thought.
We decided to travel together for a month and then I
left for home.
I was so upset. He seemed so cold the last day. He
hardly spoke. I thought well what a waste of time.
He is ruining all the nice times we had with his dog
humour now we would only remember this. We
went out to a café on the last evening for a pot of
tea.
There was a work do on. Lots of friends, laughing
and talking at the tables around us. And we, like two

wet rags hanging onto the table, with nothing to say. What a miserable site.

Then the music, which was only in the background, inspired the people at the neighbouring table to get up and dance. There wasn't much space between the tables but that didn't stop them raising up their skirts and dancing seductively around the place, the atmosphere was bubbling. More and more couples took to the floor. The music was turned up, the tables drawn back, the front door was locked and now suddenly it was a wild party and even we the two misery buckets were in full swing to the "gypsy kings".

At the end of the night when we went to pay the 57 cent for our tea, the guy said, "well you got good value for money". We had to laugh, it had been the best night of the trip.

The airport the following day wasn't quite so cheery. On the way to the airport suddenly I remembered that I had to pay the airport tax when you check in which is very unusual but I didn't have any money left. On the street my young lover stopped, took out his accordian and played a half hour and I had the tax money in my hand. If only life could always be so easy. I promised to write. He said, he would if he could. I opened the card he gave me on the plane and bawled, startling the man beside me. But with all the emotion, I couldn't explain how lovely the card had been and it made me miss my new found love all the more.

A month later when I finally got home there was a bundle of letters for me, one for every day I had been gone and my mother was seriously worried.

Clear blue but cloudy

How can a baby develop from such unloving sex. He was abusive in all ways yet I couldn't stay away from him. Something about him drew me back. I was young and naïve. But I was one of the unlucky ones that get caught. It could happen to anyone and has but maybe in other countries there is more preparation for the sexual part of life. More information. More help when things go wrong. But not where I come from. If you saw how my family react on other issues, you would know how scared I was when I found out I was pregnant. I should run and get help. Get rid of this growth. But something inside has stirred me and I feel such an attachment to this little one. But no. He, would always be connected to me if I go through with the pregancy. My family would disown me. I am not grown up enough yet. I am not financially independent. But this baby would love me. It would be close to me. I would cherish it with all my heart. I can't get rid of it. All the things I know but none of it is of help now. How will I get to the clinic? How will I keep my parents in the dark? Will it hurt? How will I be afterwards. I can't sleep. This will damage the baby. But hold on a minute I am not keeping it.

So I made my decision I had to go. There wasn't really a choice. Time was ticking and every moment the baby was growing.

The clinic was like any other. The nurses chatted insignificant chit chat and there I was being sent into a world of unconciousness, facing the most dramatic day of my life. I woke up crying. Knowing it was gone. Knowing I couldn't reverse things now. I felt empty sitting there with other girls. Each one locked in their own world. Each with the own thoughts of relief or sadness or fear. For me I was far from home. Aching in every way. No one to hug. No one to tell. Bury it deep inside.

This dead love I carried around for 10 years within me. It still aches but I have forgiven myself my mistakes. I realise that I did the best I could in the situation. News and views of baby scans ripped me apart at the beginning. Sometimes I felt lonely for my little one. I surround myself with heat in bed. I long for something warm to fill this hollow space inside me where once he dwelt so many years ago.

Clear blue
We had had such a fantastic weekend. He was
working away from home. I was so excited to see
him. I could have run the whole way if I could have
ran on water. Luckily there was a reasonable priced
flight so that did the job.
We couldn't keep our hands off each other. The
constant pull on all parts of my body. I was electric,
with wanting him. They always say it's the man who
wants the woman more physically. What do they
know?
I wanted him. I needed him. I didn't care what could
happen. He wanted to stop but how could we now. It
felt so right. We knew each other so well.
I sit here still glowing still smiling in every part of
me…
Oh no. I thought this could happen. How will I tell
anybody. Maybe it will go away. Maybe I won't
have to deal with this now. Not just now.
I should ring him first. See what he thinks.
He is really fine about it. A bit worried but fine. I am
reassured. I knew he would be ok.
It is just the rest of the crew. They are so traditional.
They love my boyfriend but will that change now???
It did. Worse than I expected. They don't want to
know me. I have gone from being loved to being a
source of shame. How can they be so hypocritical
with their beliefs? Their love of God and their
despise of me. I am not a bad person. I had thought
they would help me when I needed them most but

they turned their backs on me. Let me wallow in my
so called sin.
Months of worry. I had to go away. I left to be with
him. I had nothing. I felt so alone. He was off
working all day. Here I am totally alone. Thousands
of people around me but no friend, no familiar face.

No chance
He was my brother. My only brother. We had fought
and made up since we were small. The competition
was always enormous. The jostling and constant
tension between us was our companion always. But
now he is gone. I never got to tell him how much he
meant to me. His absence is a hole in my world. He
went out last Saturday evening with the local lads.
He was on the back of the motorbike. The dangerous
seat. I don't think they had been drinking. They were
far from home. As they came round the bend in the
road his friend lost control of the bike and they slid
off onto the road. But my dear brother hit the railing
pole and he is dead. I don't have another chance. I
can't make it up to him. We argued the week before,
something silly but of course each of us not giving
in. Both of us so sure we were right. Same as it
always was. It seems so irrelevant now but I talk to
him in my head. I want to see his face intact
forgiving me. I want him to say it is ok. But he is not
there and I won't ever be able to fight with him
again. I just fight with myself and regret our silly
squabbles.

Fireworks

People had been gathering all day beneath those massive old trees. The green space there filling up with families and friends from all over the city. Each patch of grass was soon filled with multi-coloured blankets. Food packed out or kept hidden in any bit of shade that was available.

The chatting and laughing grew as more and more people arrived. Hoots of laughter and big hugs. All in good form and delighted to see each other. One big picnic. People were friendly greeting unexpected arrivals and chance meetings. People waving urgently trying to get each others attention. Steering towards their pals but bumping into old friends on the way.

As most of the space had been filled the atmosphere quietened and there was the lovely hum of people eating chatting and laughing.

The stage was being prepared. Nobody much noticed at the beginning but as the settings on the stage became more elaborate and the microphones were being tested. Everyone's attention started to be directed towards the front.

The music began and everyone rose to see the performers. Wow what a beginning. Everybody was so mellow now from being in the hot sun with wine and food all day. People lay back listening feeling their senses overflow with warmth. The beauty of it all.

The sky darkened as the flying foxes left the trees and an eerie feeling seeped into the crowd. It was

like being part of a film. The music chased the
emotions of our hearts around. Teasing out all
hidden losses and fears and love and lost love and
leaving even the toughest man weak.
The final scenes and the music build up with the
crowd again on their feet. Men and women weeping
and children hugging. And then the sky lit up. Lit up
in every colour imaginable. Last claps and hisses.
Dramatic and fantastic the crowd were awed.
Mouths left hanging. Tears still pouring down
nobody cared anymore how they looked. Everybody
in love with that evening and with love with those
around them. Stilled and sighing with wonder.
Music and fireworks, family and friends, drowning
in it and loving it.

No time for goodbye
I passed by the house. I could have called in but I
wanted to get home. It had been a great weekend but
I was tired. This was the time before mobile phones.
Can you remember? It is not that long ago. So when
I got in the door. There were so many messages on
the answering machine. All with the same message.
Ring home. With a heavy sigh and a sickening
feeling in my stomach, I picked up the phone and
dialled the number. Waiting for an answer all the
possible scenarios ran through my head. But I tried
to calm myself saying I don't always have to think
the worst. Eventually my mother answered the
phone. Oh dear. I knew in her voice something was
wrong. My dear dad was dead. He had died at
around the time that I passed the house. God, I was
torn. I felt so bad. Like all my energy had sunk to
my feet. My poor mother. She had witnessed my dad
excruciated by the pain ripping through his heart.
The blood in his mouth. He went so fast. She wasn't
ready. Whoever is? I certainly am not. I dragged
myself back into the car and drove in a daze home.
All those miles back again. All those miles bringing
me back to the harsh reality that my mother is now
alone in that big house. My father is gone. My
sisters away and although I am living in the same
country I am still so far away. If I had known that I
only had one more chance to see my father I would
have called in. I wouldn't have minded the droning
chit chat. I would be treasuring it now.

Blue Morning - Red Sunset

You think that I might have forgotten you my little one. I never will. You lived in me for a while. I was full of you. We had the twins a while and I was delighted to be pregnant again. I enjoyed being pregnant. Feeling you growing in me. First it was our big secret. It's funny being with people you know well and they don't know that you have another little person with you. Everybody noticed I was in great form. The slight nausea and tiredness hadn't got to me as much this time as I knew it was part of the package.

I was really nervous about the first scan. Terrified that there would be something wrong with the baby or even that it might be twins. I was so relieved when they said it was only one baby. A beautiful baby with all its parts intact. I was thrilled. Delighted and excited.

Funny thing is when I came home and looked at the scans I found them disturbing in some strange way. I felt very strange. I took all but one of the photos down.

The next day in work I still didn't feel quite myself. The sad stories of my client really got to me and I myself felt caught up in her sadness.

I needed a hug, reassurance. I felt raw and vulnerable. Nobody was there for me.

And then I needed even more reassurance when I made my way to the toilet and discovered I was bleeding. The maternity unit of the hospital wouldn't see me. It is too early at 13 wks. So I made my way

to the accident and emergency part of the hospital.
And you know what it is like there. Hours of
waiting. Hours of holding on. Hoping that I was not
losing my baby.
Then that horrible woman, how could you call her a
nurse? She made me feel the whole thing was my
fault when I told her that the only unusual thing was
that the day before I had to race after the buggy one
of the twins had pushed down the hill which was
heading straight for my other twin.
She had already made up her mind that my by now
slight cramps were caused by my reckless
behaviour, which meant a threatened miscarriage.
So I was glad when I met with the young doctor who
at least compensated for his lack of knowledge or
experience with his gentle kind manner. A passing
nurse mentioned that miscarriage was nature's way
to get rid of something that is not viable, that it often
happened and that it didn't meant that no other child
could be conceived. I thought it was odd her saying
these things and smiled and nodded politely but
somewhat felt that what she was saying to me didn't
apply to my situation.
I was sent home.
The next day was the usual chaos with twin toddlers.
But that evening wasn't good. The cramps were so
strong now I headed to bed at 6. At one in the
morning it was inevitable that my little baby was
leaving. The pain and discomfort was all too
familiar. I had to let him go.

When I headed to the toilet I felt a big swoosh
between my legs and there dangling on the cord was
my little baby only the size of my hand. I screamed
in anguish. My husband came rushing. Nothing
could have prepared him for that sight. He was fixed
to the spot mouth agasp. Get the scissors and a bowl.
I can't just stand here forever. And he did the job,
severing the connection of me with our little baby. I
had imagined it differently. It broke our hearts,
everything 6 months too early. My husband
wandered around forlornly with the bowl with the
little fella looking like it was just sleeping.
What do you do in this situation? It is not something
anybody ever talks about. Nothing that you learn in
school can prepare you.
And so I landed back in the hospital. With shock and
disgust marked all over the faces meeting me when
they saw what was in the bowl. And as lay bleeding
there for all I was worth. Nobody came. I had time
to say goodbye. I cried and prayed and reflected.
Eventually it was time to go home. My little one
would be cremated at our request. The young doctor
from the day before met me by chance with tears in
his eyes. I was so glad for someone to acknowledge
my pain. Someone connected to their heart.
I left the hospital empty in so many ways. There
must be thousands of women out there feeling or
having felt like me. How come I know nothing about
this?

Married

The wedding party

I am determined it will be the best wedding ever.
None of these boring hours, where nobody knows
what to say or do. There will be people coming from
all over. Friends and family scattered to the wind
reunited. Most of my friends don't know each other
or the family.

I got the bunch of raffle tickets. Everyone arriving
would get one. And then we bought the prizes.
Ridiculous things, anything to get the atmosphere
going, have a bit of a laugh. Luckily my wife has a
sense of humour.

We decided to get a lady in who would show
everyone how to do our traditional dancing. She
could walk around with the microphone giving
instructions. It might be disastrous. But we have to
risk it. The people I know are mostly game for a
laugh.

My wife said she would wear a suit she wasn't into
all the meringue dresses. To tell you the truth I don't
give a damn what she wears. She is gorgeous
anyway. Everybody loves her.

I am her number one fan.

So we are all set. All organised. Nearly everyone we
invited is coming.

The wedding march begins. I turn in my seat to see
my bride in her suit wondering what colour it will be
and there she is in the shortest mini wedding dress I
have ever seen. God I have to keep control of
myself. She is a stunner. The priest has managed to

keep upright and has managed to close his mouth before she gets to the altar with her Dad. I can't stop laughing from nervousness. The gasps of the guests have subsided but everyone is grinning. She is a divil. Her and her suit… Well she has certainly set the tone for the day. Hilarious and full of surprises.

Displaced

I woke up in the small dark room. I didn't want to
look. I didn't want to know that this was our new
home. How could it be? There was nothing here
familiar to me. My family and friends thousands of
miles away. My language only on the tip of my
tongue but not of those in these neighbourhoods.
The landscape so close not stretching for miles into
the distance. My clothes - where can I buy the same
again? If I wear them, people will laugh at me.
I was respected. I had people to help me look after
my children. I had people to help in the kitchen and
farm work. I never had to cart trolley loads of food
from the shops. My arms will surely reach the
ground soon from all the heaving and shoving of
great weights.
I can't go back. I can't ever see my family again. We
would be killed if we took a step on the soil I love
and treasure in my heart.
I married him knowing he was different. Knowing
that my family didn't approve. He wrote important
documents. He hung around with intellectuals who
could see the mistakes being made. The
discrimination. He felt strongly enough to put pen to
paper. Now we are here. I did not wish for this
lonliness. I did not wish for this isolation. I can't see
the people I love, wed. I mourn alone when
somebody dies in my homeland.
Everyday I wake up another part of my body is
aching. The doctors cannot find anything wrong

with me. The sadness spreads in me, inhabiting each
cell.
I have made friends here now. I have studied hard.
Now I can speak the local language. I can even
laugh at their jokes.
But it is not home.

Adult

Let go
Can you come with me please? Very strange I
thought. What is up? It was unusual for my boss to
call me for a meeting at this time of the morning. I
was straight back off my holidays. We had had a
wonderful time. I was really relaxed after the months
of previous stress in work.
He looked so serious. Very uptight. I wondered if he
had found out something about our new competitors.
I was supposed to contact them after the holidays.
Then the bombshell dropped.
I should start looking for a job. What now. Sorry I
am so confused. You said I could stay till the end,
that I knew the ins and outs of all sides of the
business.
Yes but you are responsible for a family. You need
to start looking now. So that you can be guaranteed
of getting something that is enough to support you
and the family.
I know it is to my benefit. But I feel so wrenched
apart. So torn between his concern for my welfare
on the one hand and the feeling of absolute
uselessness on the other. I took my job seriously. I
invested so much energy into it. I knew we would be
closing at some stage. But not everyone was gone
yet. It was so hard to be told I wasn't t needed any
more.
I felt very old. Ancient, sad, lost in myself.

Suddenly I felt that I had had no holiday at all. How would I tell my husband who was struggling with his own life?
I left the room stunned. The others around me were shocked too. It was a new beginning for me I guess but it just was a very tough time then.

The worlds waiting for you

"Good morning. Can you come to my office, please." "Oh dear. Am I going to be one of the 150 people to be let go". I flushed hot and cold in seconds. I don t know what to think.

Should I be happy or sad? I hated this job in so many ways. I would be obvious target, one of the last into the company. Paid well for a job that is not essential. Cut backs everywhere. I would cut this job too in their position.

So in I sat in the hot seat. When I saw the personnel officer in the room too then I knew that I would definitely be let go.

They were so nice. That is what made me cry. I knew they were as nervous as I was. How could I be anything but nice back to them?

But as I really took it in, I realised I was exhausted. I didn't know what I really wanted to do. I wanted to start a totally different career. But I am bordering on being" past it" and by the time I would be finished studying it probably wouldn't be worth it. I also have family to look after both financially and on a daily basis. I don't have the time or the money required.

The thought of putting everything together to look for a job, the constant battle to present yourself in the correct way so that employers will want to take you, the effort of it all, running side and side with family life, it made me very weary. The worry that now that there are not so many jobs to be had that

maybe this one was better than I thought and I should have put more of an effort in.
And they looked at me trying to figure out what was spinning around in my head. I laughed and cried simultaneously totally red in the face now. I left the room, numb embarrassed, knowing that everyone who passed me in the corridor would know that I was one of the 150. I really did feel like a loser with a package in my hand of all the possibilities my life held for me. I just had to have the strength to grab them.

Sleep

Sleep, such a special word, something you probably
take for granted. Just as you can go to the toilet, you
can sleep. I am not one of those lucky ones. You
probably don't even count yourself lucky.

I lie down and what happens I wake up. I might as
well have a stick of dynamite under my bottom.
Suddenly I am so full of energy. In fact I think I
could rip out the contents of this house and fling it
out the top window.

Relax. I have done everything possible. We have got
rid of our television. I don't drink alcohol much,
don't smoke, don't drink coffee, avoid social contact
in the evenings, avoid late meals, strenuous activity
before bed, the list goes on. I have tried every
relaxing technique you have ever heard of. And
where does it get me?

Tablets, yes I have tried a great variety, to no avail. I
need to be able to function the following day.
Dependency on tablets is not something I want.

I went to a doctor with a knee injury once and she
asked me if I was a top athlete. I laughed at her. I try
my best to stay awake during the day and don't run
marathons. But my muscle structure is that of an
athlete. Non-stop tension gives that to you, I
suppose. Every situation has its advantages I
thought.

I do sleep sometimes. So what is the problem? The
problem is that when I sleep I want it to continue so
that I can feel refreshed. But you can't have family,

a job and friends and not sleep for a week and then sleep a week.

I am sure you know what it is to worry about something and toss and turn the night through. And you with children know what it is like to get up regularly at all hours of the night and maybe find it hard to go back to sleep. But life moves on and kids get bigger but here I still am years later waiting to sleep.

Wasted

Do you want to meet in town for a drink? Oh, how I would love to go. Love to head out without a care in the world. Love even to go out to moan. But I had one or two things this week. A trip to the doctor, a long telephone conversation and I am so exhausted. I can't risk it. I know it sounds ridiculous to you. You look at me and think what in god's name is wrong with her. She doesn't even look sick. But take a trip inside my body and you would then know how much hell this is. Do you think that if I had a choice that I would spend all these lonely hours huddled away in this tiny flat, freezing. I can't even jump around to get my blood circulating to keep warm. It is 5 years now since I collapsed after I came home from work. Five of the best years of my life. That's what they should have been. I am not married, I have no children. I don't know if I should be grateful or not. So I came home from work. I felt like I had had a heart attack. I just couldn't do anything. The doctors came. They just said I needed rest and that I should be ok soon.

I had been great. Working hard, studying at night, really enjoying the buzz of it all. I can't really understand it. I didn't think something like this would or could happen to me. I had heard of yuppie flu and burn out syndrome and ME but what did it really mean? I didn't get better as I had expected and everybody else expected. I wasn't depressed as everybody thought I was. I mean now I get depressed, majorly depressed but not then, I just wanted my life back. Now I don't know if that will ever be. That is the worst of this illness, the not knowing, the lack of acknowledgement of how serious and debilitating this illness is.

We are a funny lot. We always think that sick people have to be disfigured in some way, spots, haggard, limping. Yet think of all the people with cancer walking around not knowing that there are massive tumours growing in them till it's too late and then suddenly the drastic look.

Well I live on here. Aching and exhausted. Eating only the best food, that I really can't afford on disability allowance. Sometimes I get so thin as I really have no appetite, I get lung infections when others get a slight cold. I have checked out every doctor, specialist, given away all my money for all types of therapies, checked out the internet and read every medical journal. And am I any the wiser. Yes in many ways I am. I appreciate everything that is of any meaning in life now. I know how precious health is. I know that only a very thin line separates the healthy and the ill. I know myself so well now. I know my limitations and my strengths. I make the most of what I have. But I really want my old life back. I want the freedom to say yes to things that I feel like without weeks in bed afterwards for any little stretching of my limits. And I want it now.

Parent

I swung my head over the toilet bowl again. Heaving
up all the goodness that should be going to my baby.
I am distraught knowing that I have been so good
eating all the right things, avoiding alcohol and
cigarette smoke. Exercising as much as possible.
And now it is all down the drain and I am empty
inside. Well not quite empty, as that little creature is
hanging on for all its worth to my insides hoping for
something more substancial. As I make my way to
the doctors, I see a beautiful flower growing out of a
crack in the pavement and it gives me hope. Maybe
my baby will survive as this flower has.
My doctor says I should be eating more greens. I
think what is the point when they will just end up in
the toilet bowl. How about some folic acid tablets
which are small enough to keep down and I can take
them when I am feeling less nauseous?
Pregnant! Isn't it fantastic news? Congratulations!
Wow that's great!
Sorry, but I don't feel at all great. 9 months of gastic
enteritis wouldn't be your idea of fun either would
it?!
But as my belly swells and I feel it kick, I can put up
with the nauseous feelings, the vomiting the cramps.
I lie in the sun with my big belly showing, proud
that we have got so far.
As I near the end and she makes her way down, I
feel like I am going on the toughest hike of my life. I
try to breathe and keep calm, knowing that the
greatest view is yet to come.

As my husband pours water on my back, he comforts me. The midwife is driving me crazy with her nervousness and instruments ready. I want space. I am ready to do this. My baby is ready too. And here she comes. Oh my God, it's a baby. The longest baby in the world. And I am laughing and crying. We are a mess in more ways than one. But we have got through the 9 months, hopefully we have the strength to get through the years.

Dependant

Ours little starfish lying in the bed beside us. I couldn't put her in the cot. I needed to hear her breathe. We went in with 2 people we have come home with three. Our world is upside down since. We are so happy, so excited but so tired. We need to get some routine. I mean she can't keep thinking night starts at 4 in the afternoon and ends at 1 in the morning. I have taken to going bed with her and getting up when my husband comes home around 9 and then sleeping again between 11 and 1. Then she is all smiles. Grinning from ear to ear and I can't help but smile though I can hardly stand up with tiredness.

As I changed her nappy last night and it was such a mess, she got sick all over her hair and that at 2 in the morning. Where should I start, I should just lie down on the carpet and cry, let her suck and shit and puke all over and when I have the energy I will wake up again in a few months and clear it all up.

But no, get a grip. This is our little girl. She needs me. She is totally and absolutely dependant on us. She cannot wait for me to get over this crisis. I have to get over it now. Clear her up, even if the process repeats in another few hours. Get up in the morning. Go to the shops and look like a normal person. Moan a bit, grin a bit and be ready for another night of the same.

The days seem so normal when we get out in the fresh air all seems well and I forget the horrors. Everybody can't help smiling when she makes her chorkling noises. Then when she starts her screaming, her heart wrenching screetch, it rips my heart out. I sweat and dive into action trying to find the cause of her ailment and hope that all those passersby can keep their comments positive because I am doing my best. I don't have a degree in this. I don't have any experience but I love my little girl and I would do anything for her.

Now
We were in such a rush. You know how it is, at the
last minute. Just when you are just getting to the car
somebody has forgotten something.The kids have a
meltdown about what shoes they don't want to wear.
My blood pressure was rising. Aah, I could explode.
Can we never get out of the house without this battle
ground?
We eventually get to the party. Tattered at the edges
but we were so dressed up maybe nobody would
notice.
My little boy was tugging at my sleeve whinging.
God, we have just arrived. What is it?
Toilet. Ok Ok.
I nearly didn't notice but just as I pulled up his
trousers I saw the swelling. All his legs right up to
the top. He was a little flushed. He had been
whinging but I had thought it was the aftermath of
the stress of getting here.
What is this? The more I looked at him the more I
knew something was wrong. I had to get help. With
all the flap of getting here, suddenly within minutes
I was leaving with him.
The doctor referred us to the hospital, more probing
and examining. More intrigued stares. This is my
son. Not some bloody spectacle. I don't need your
stares. I need your help. No, I won't go home and
leave my son in your capable hands. He is only 3.
Do you know how frightened I am? Can you even
begin to imagine how frightened he is? And you ask
me to go home and leave him here in a strange place

with people he doesn't know when he is at his most vulnerable.

We will get to the bottom of this. I am not leaving until I get a proper answer.

Transferred to another hospital. More tests and probing. My darling good boy. You will be ok. I am here for you. Oh please just make him better. Please now.

And the diagnosis. A very rare childrens illness that can damage the heart and other organs if not treated in time. He can be treated. It will help but he will continue to have symtoms, pain but it will disappear with time.

Now everytime he is not well, I worry that it is back again. I wonder what's going on in his body that I can't see. Then I forget again, watch him laugh and kick that ball again. Watch him and treasure him.

Natural?

We have been trying for years. Yes, literally years and no seed has taken to my rich and willing soil. I feel useless and depressed. I try to motivate myself to the whole procedure. That is what life has become. My every thought rotates around my fertility, my infertility. I try so hard not to try so hard. In normal people's lives they just get pregnant whether they want to or not. Why not me? They have checked us both out. We have all our bits in working order. So why won't even one little egg get fertilized? We both have so much to offer. We would love the child so much. We love even the thought of the child. I can see it in my arms but the test again is negative. No blue line. Others would be relieved but I am not. I want a little baby, our own flesh and blood. How can it be so hard? Is it not natural? What is wrong with me? Would other people know to look at me that I am so desperate? It hurts to look at other women cuddling their babies on the buses, in the cafes everywhere I turn. And when a man holds his child to his chest I want to cry out with the pain of it. I know my husband is suffering too. He would love a child as much as I would but the last few months he is withdrawing from me as I become more obsessive and nervy and snappy. I don't think he wants a kid as much as I do anymore and it makes me mad. But we have to be relaxed and love each other or it will never work out. It is all getting a bit too much for me now. The strain is taking its toll. If a baby comes now I will be a physical and mental wreck. Please let it come soon.

Alone

We weren't married long and I was pregnant.
Although I was feeling a bit nauseous I was excited
as well. It was all new, husband, house and now
baby on the way. I had had many boyfriends, had
romanced a bit about what it would be like being
married. But somehow this wasn't the picture I had
in mind. I wasn't the type of girl to be swept away
by a man on a white horse. I wanted to have a good
friend and lover as a husband. But I have this. A
man who insists his dinner is on the table when he
gets in from work, a man who cannot understand
what I would be doing all day in the house. Doesn't
he know how long it takes to decide what wallpaper,
curtains, sofa etc go together? Doesn't he want to
chat and know what sort of thoughts are going on in
my head? I used to hang out with my pals in work.
Have a laugh. I felt funny, intelligent, interesting.
Now I am growing bigger by the moment. Losing
my figure, losing my funniness, no one interested in
me or my intelligence. I am trapped inside these four
walls with a dog of a husband. Who should I talk to?
I can't talk to my family or friends. It is too private.
I don't know the neighbours yet. But they don't look
like my type of person. How could I have waited so
long for this? Saved myself for this man? How can
an intelligent woman get herself into this situation?
It wasn't a marriage set by my parents. But they
liked him too. If you want to know me come and
live with me they say. Well maybe there is

something to be said for that but in my time that was
definitely not allowed.

Appreciated

Every morning I get up to a new day delighted that I have this job where I feel appreciated and I can get things done. I started here when I was only a young lad and I have worked my way up slowly but surely doing any exams they have put in my way. I have it tough sometimes working long hours out on the road mending broken lines and not knowing where the next call will bring me. But that is part of the draw of this job. The sense of adventure, the carry on with the lads either in the early morning when we are half asleep or in the evenings when we pop into the pub for a quick one.

Many of us have young families. We are earning the money so they can grow. I am involved in my job just as my wife is involved in hers. We don't know much about what each of us are doing during the day. But we are chugging along nicely.

I love tackling the job at hand. Looking to find out what the problem is. Taking the measurements, doing test runs and getting all going again. It's a great sense of achievement. Having people call you up with a problem and giving them a call later to tell them everything is back in working order again. Most of my bosses have been fairly decent. The odd fella was tough and cantankerous. But I know how to keep busy and out of their way. I don't provoke them. I keep my head down. Some say I am a real softie but when I see the trouble they get into I am not enthusiastic to change.

Food glorious food

She has the food everywhere. What is the point of putting out a spoon for her? She loves her food. Not the baby food that we give her in her bowl but our dinners. When we are not looking she grabs food off our plates and stuffs it in her mouth. Her tiny little fist oozing with food. Her grin from ear to ear.

It is never a problem with pieces of potato or meat but you should see her eating spaghetti. We only laugh making her enjoy it all the more. We aren't strict on table manners yet. There is plenty of time for that. She has a fist full of spaghetti with tomato sauce. She manages to get quite a bit of it into her mouth. Some of it falls back on the plate more is on the table and the floor. We have plastic sheeting around her chair. It is only when she decides to rub her head and discovers the new sensation that we realise that maybe it would be easier to feed her in the bath.

But what joy. She loves it. I have never seen someone enjoy their food so much but I have also never seen such a mess.

Wake up, sleepy head

It was such a rush this morning. Her little head soft on the pillow. She was as warm as new bread. It wrenched me open, touching her, to wake her up. It wasn't natural. She could have slept another hour at least. I eventually managed to wake her. We sat snuggled together on the bed. I slowly eased her out of her pyjammas and into her fresh new clothes. She smelled so good. As her warmth left me and she made her way to the toilet I thought of how vulnerable she was. She is really strong. She can wrap me round her finger. She can roar like no small animal when things do not suit her but in the morning hours when she is soft and bedraggled she is my baby and I feel it in my whole body. I want to protect her. I want her to have it easy.

Spooning the food into herself she is gettting excited now. Realising what day it is. The first day of a whole new life. A life outside these four walls. A life where I won't be there.

I am relieved that she is a bit more awake.

I have looked forward to having the time to myself but worry about how she will be with the new teacher and what the other kids in her class will be like. Will she be bullied? Will she make friends easily?

The clocks flies round and in the last mad dash we get our coats and shoes on and I don't have anymore time to be dreaming and worrying. I don't want her to be late on her first day.

And there they are, all the other mammys, daddys and kids. All hand in hand. The kids break free to catch up with pals and little by little the worry falls away. Knowing we all survived and she will survive too.

However the emptiness in the house when I return, the stillness, is enormous. In some ways it is what I dreamed of, but I let myself have a little cry, knowing that things have moved on, my little girl is growing up and I can grow too.

The climb
Exhilarating is all I can say. We headed off this
morning just as the sun came up. There wasn't much
talk out of us on the cable car up. It seemed to go on
forever and I thought there wouldn't be much of a
climb after that. But when we got out I could see
those snowy peaks stretching up to the sky.
Disappearing in and out of the early morning fog.
They predicted a glorious day. And it was. The fog
lifted soon after we arrived and everything dewy
glistened in the sunshine. I felt all caught up with
emotion. Yes, it was so, so beautiful. I was a bit
breathless, my blood pressure felt like it was down
around my ankles. We were marching over snow
fields now. I could have rolled in it like a puppy and
yelped with delight. Trudging along step by step we
got nearer to the top. We were so high up now. It
was like being in a plane. Sometimes fluffy clouds
from below snuck up along the wall of the mountain
and surprised us by rising up like billows of white
smoke out of a big chimney.
Rooks flew overhead gliding and swerving in the
wind currents. Letting us know this was their place
and we were just visitors, so we should behave.
And then we were at the top. Purple in the face, but
glowing. We had made it. Sweaty and sticky, but
freezing in the wind coming over the ice. I wanted to
drink the view in. I just couldn't get enough.
But we couldn't stay long in the freezing cold. The
sun was beating down hard but did little to warm us.
As we turned each corner around each rock was

another view. Another lake of intense green or blue. What is hiking? Walking on solid ground in the sky. Feeling like you are flying high with the emotion of having made it. We weren't alone, so many had made it out today to push themselves and get the prize. Kids and grannies included. I hope I will continue to be strong enough to do these hikes for many years to come.

Down
I have known her for years. She has had her bouts of
depression. She hadn't been great the last while. But
I thought she would recover as many times before.
We are all exhausted not knowing how to help her.
She has been years on medication now. But nothing
really helps in the long run. She is always full of
hope when she starts a new drug, thinking it will be
the one, the one to give her life back, the one that
will make a difference.
When she is up, she is great. So full of life and
hilarious. Maybe it's 'cos she doesn't have the same
barriers as we do maybe she sees life differently. I
didn't realise she had a problem when I met her. We
were in college together and you only see each other
when things are good. It was after we left college
and we got to see each other more regularly. We
cooked together and sometimes I stayed over. I
noticed that sometimes she was ragged. Torn in
herself. I know we all have our moments but this
was different. It didn't change much over the years.
There were good and bad times but more
increasingly a frustration on her part that she wasn't
moving on in life. Everything was stagnant. She was
sick of trying. The effort was just too much.
And so this morning I got the news. I wanted to
throw up. To throw up everything within me. I just
don't want to know that I wasn't there to help her.
That she died a terrible death. A very deliberate
death. A death that has shocked so many others even
those not related to her. Her life was dramatic and

her death too. Oh why, why did it have to end like this?

Party
You know it felt like when I was small. I would
make lists of things to buy for our parties after our
sales of work. Now I was doing it for real. Thinking
of what I could bake. What would everybody like to
eat. And the music. Hours of putting together tapes
of all the oldies. Making sure there was something
for everyone. Build up the atmosphere.
Then the invitations.
"Take a break from the everyday routine. Dress up
and party. Wear something funny".
This was the first party I had organised here (except
childrens parties- and I had always enjoyed them).
I only invited friends and neighbours that I knew
were not too embarressed to let loose, go a bit nuts
on a Sunday afternoon.
It rained buckets and I was never so glad. Then most
people would have nothing better to do than come
along. And they were dressed up. Not ball gowns,
that sort of thing. But hilarious wigs, funny noses,
masks and war paint. It was great.
We hugged and laughed. We ate and drank.
Whirling around between all these great people who
make my life so great here in my new homeland.
We played traditional music first. I had to show
them the moves to begin with. Then there was no
stopping them. They were stamping and twirling,
squeeling and aching with laughter.
Everybody was up. We changed the music. Back to
those old days. And we went nuts. Making use of the
full length of the hall. Some were a bit shy but they

had plenty to laugh at as the lads shook their heads till their wigs fell off to some heavy metal. Swinging hips. Bouncing people. Kids jumping from the stage. Joining in and hiding again behind the curtain. They had their own party up there as their parents became kids again on the dancefloor.

Needed

I am still standing here on the side of the pitch. The years have gone by. Rain has lashed me, Sun has burnt me. I have cheered on their team with all my heart and now he is no longer a small fella in shorts too long. He is a young man. A young man ready to finish school. Still playing football twice a week. What am I doing here you may ask? I am standing here with his inhaler. When he gets exhausted sometimes he is just gasping for air and he panics, can't get the breathing right, can't focus and relax enough to do it for himself. I have to be there to calm him down. He is gasping now. He is running towards me I have the inhaler primed. I encourage him firmly but gently. Nobody stares any more. They have seen it all before. I will always be there looking out for him.

Hurt
Yes, I am just the woman you see collecting the kids
from the kindergarten. You see me everyday but you
don't know what my eyes have seen.
You look at the television and see the headlines. To
you, who have never experienced any real terror,
you don't realise that I experienced a scene like that
not that long ago. I was the leading actress but I
couldn't take off the costumes afterwards, wipe the
makeup off and walk away. I have to live with the
marks of those headlines in my body. The memories
of what my eyes have seen are etched on my brain. I
am comfortable with my daily routines here. I am
glad to be alive though sometimes I wish I could
have gone with the rest of them to an early grave so
I wouldn't have to carry the memory of their
anguished faces with me.

Bags packed
I can still see their faces imprinted on my mind. Still
set their on the dock as they waved me goodbye. I
may never see them again. There are so few of them
left now. Many dead, from the fighting or the
hunger. Their hunger has sculpted their faces.
I will get a job. I will get money enough to feed
them. I will get out of here. Get a new life. Not have
to fear each day for my life.
The boat is full, full of hopeful souls and hungry
faces. We are all in this together but we are so alone.
Alone in our hearts not knowing if we will ever
return, not knowing if we will ever want to. The soil
drenched with too many sad memories. The happy
memories smothered by the sorrow. I can't stay and
see everything that we own and love disappear.

I could pack my bags today. I have had enough of
this. I just don't belong here. It is just not the same
as home. I just can't share a joke with any person I
meet, in the shop or on the street. First, the words
come out in such a jumble and second, they don't
understand my sense of humor. What is the point of
our relationship when he understands everything
here? He grew up here, each place has a meaning to
him. I am lost. I mean you could look on it as an
adventure. That is how I saw it at the beginning but
now well the novelty has worn off. He goes to work.
I can do what I want. I can wander around aimlessly.
I don't know anyone except him. I feel like an idiot
everytime I open my mouth. I am an intelligent

being but you wouldn't think that if you heard me.
You think I hadn't a brain in my head.
Sometimes we meet up with his friends or family.
They are all very nice and friendly but it is only
normal that they want to be able to have a
conversation. And so as the evening goes on I can
understand less and less as their conversations get
more animated, their memories don't include me and
my opinions and memories swim round in my head
trying to find the right words to express them but
then the conversation has moved on to the next
theme and I stay lost in my world with a blank face
smiling and nodding and feeling very, very lonely.

I got their joke. Imagine that I could laugh on cue.
Not a half an hour after everybody else. This is a call
for celebration. Do you know how long I have
dreamed of this moment? Years and years of
listening to their stories. Years of not being able to
share their laughter. Years of wanting to join in.
Next thing you know, I will be telling my own jokes
and stories and they will be laughing. That is what I
call success.

I am serving you cheese at the cheese counter, or
cleaning your floors or sweating in that big kitchen.
Do you know how hard I studied in my homeland?
Do you know how much it cost my parents to get me
through college? They saved every penny to give me

a life better than their own. But the war changed
everything. We had to flee. We had to get out of
there in a hurry. Anywhere, just run.
We didn't have time to collect all our papers.
Everything was burning. The clothes on our backs
we were lucky to have.
Now I cannot earn my money the easy way. I have
to start from scratch again. I have to learn this
language. I have n't the money to study. I could not
sit the exams in this country. My language would
never be good enough. And you never really look at
me. I was respected as a good doctor in my country.
People looked up to me, knew that I could help them
in their pain.
I know how to examine you and find out what is
wrong with you but that is no use if I cannot explain
to you what the problem is and you cannot make
yourself understood to me.
Someday, perhaps.

Salt on the wind

The ocean is belting the sand on this shore. The waves roll their glistening heads forward to crash down again. The salt wind fills my lungs and I pull my hood up against its biting force.

I have nestled down in the rocks and gaze eternally at these waves. Over and over. There is no rush today. Nothing to do but just be here. So few days in my life like this. As I get a bit cold I struggled to stand upright again. I realise when I stand up that I am frozen to the bone. I run along the beach. Arms stretched up to the sky. Running and laughing like a maniac. There is no one here to see me. I laugh at the madness of it all. Even if someone was here they wouldn't hear me with the roar of the waves. I run and run till I feel the blood rushing in my veins. My heart is pumping hard and I can hardly catch my breath with the wind. I slow down. The sun is coming out now. Its rays dancing on the surface. It looks like it isn't sure if it is coming out or not. The wind is stronger now and it seems to blow the heavy rain clouds away. I roll up my trousers, slip off my socks and shoes and edge my way into the ripples at the water's edge. It is bloody freezing but refreshing. I trot off again. Dodging the bigger waves and letting the ripples of water and the sand tickle my feet. I spot a lovely shell and duck to pick it up. The wave catches me off guard and the ends of my trousers are soaking now. The seagulls are squeaching with laughter. And so they might, seeing this crazy human enjoy the wildness of the day. I never tire of this water's edge. Every day it is different, the light, the waves, the sand. I have my wonderland here by the sea.

Let go
She let me go today. I didn't see it coming. She was always so positive and strong. I know we had our ups and downs, who doesn't? But when I came home today she was gone with the kids. No forwarding address. I have always done my best but it wasn't good enough. I love my kids just as much as she does. But now I have no choice, my life in tatters overnight. I think about the larger questions in life. I worry about the state of the world and all this time she had obviously being worrying about the state of our marriage. But she never said.
How threatening am I in her eyes that she didn't have the courage to say that she was going? How much of a coward is she? How much of a coward am I now to face this life without her and the kids. To know, that she may find another. To know that maybe my kids will grow up with some other father figure by their sides.
Today is not a good day.

~~~~~~~~~~~~~~~~~~~~~~~~~~~~~~~~

I am aching to see her to feel her embrace. To see her glow and know I am welcome. We have been together for several weeks now. The excitement is amazing. At first I thought I would explode with my heart pumping so much. My eyes darting to all sides expecting to be caught. She isn't younger than my wife, it isn't her looks that attracted me, it was her interest in me. She is absorbed with me as much as I with her. We want each other. At home all is fine we
~~~~~~~~~~~~~~~~~~~~~~~~~~~~~~~~

just chug along from day to day. But there is no excitement. No interest. We are bored with each other. She has the kids and all their stories. She has her pals and all their stories. Sometimes I think she doesn't even know I exist. She never seems to see me. Never looks at me longingly. Now that I have other interests I don't feel as angry with her for ignoring me. In fact I am really pleased as she doesn't seem to notice me at all. We are getting along a bit better as I am in better form. I have to be careful though as sometimes I am so excited I nearly tell her. I don't think that would help at all.

~~~~~~~~~~~~~~~~~~~~~~~~~~~~~~~~~~

She has found someone else. She, who was my young bride. We had two lovely children together and then one day she was gone. The ache in my heart has not healed. It gets worse. She has got on with her life. Our girls are almost teenagers. I caught one of them calling him Daddy. How could they? Am I nothing to them even though their genes tell another story? Their lives are so full of school and friends. Why would they want to come to me.That was ok when they were small. I don't even have the financial pull. They can't even come to me asking for money.

~~~~~~~~~~~~~~~~~~~~~~~~~~~~~~~~~~

My phone is the same as his. That's why I reached for it when it signalled a text had arrived. I couldn't grasp it first. "I really miss you". But nobody I know would be missing me. All who are close to me are here in this room. Slowly, it dawned on me. Shit, this is not my phone and worse, someone is missing my husband while I am with him.

~~~~~~~~~~~~~~~~~~~~~~~~~~~~~~~~~~~~~~~

I can't live with these divided feelings. I should give up my thoughts about him. We were just work mates but things just developed. I didn't make choices but in doing so I have ended up in this mess. My husband now knows I just haven't been myself. I cannot lie. He can read me like a book. Alcohol of course played a role in the changing scenes of our relationship. It brought things to a level I had fantasized about but thought that is what they would remain. Now it is too late to turn back the clocks. I am sick with worry and disgust of how I let things happen. I didn't mean to hurt anyone. I acted on my feelings.

~~~~~~~~~~~~~~~~~~~~~~~~~~~~~~~~~~~~~~~

I couldn't take another day of your abuse and rages. Your binges on alcohol made you another person. We used to drink together when we were younger. But over the years I had to take the responsibility for family life as you didn't or couldn't. You always wanted more from me. You needed our love like a bandage for a sore head. But no more. I will not be your crutch. I will not be your victim. Go find someone else to abuse.

You know what has made it so hard to come to this stage. I know the other side of you. I know the intelligent, funny, warm side of you. I just wish that I could experience it more often. We have tried. We really have, for our family's sake, tried to patch things up, to make things better. I am worn out now. I don't have another ounce of strength left in me, so just go.

I would leave her if I could. Her stinging comments. Her lack of warmth or care for anyone but herself or her kids. Yes, I call them her kids. But I love them too. She has them all day when I am out of work and she has poisoned them with her version of me. I know she bitches about me when I am not here. I see it in the way the kids react to me. They are not as welcoming as they used to be. I have become more involved in my work. That is where I feel well. I feel appreciated and people acknowledge that I have done a good job. Here I just feel that I need to bring in the money so they can get on with their lives without me. I can fix things that are broken. But this relationship has been long broken. Now it is just habit. I get up, go out to work arrive home to a messy house, a moaning wife and kids that are busy with their homework or friends. I plonk in front of the telly. News of anything that is not happening here, is good news. It is a diversion. I nod off and wake up to the call for dinner. There isn't much conversation at the table so I head inside and look at the telly. Soon it is time to go to bed. I need to be up early in the morning. She can stay up half the night as she doesn't have to perform fully in the morning. What are we doing? Hanging on to this marriage? Hanging on to this life? But to tell you the truth, I don't have the energy or inclination to change. What else is there anyway? I don't want to rock the boat. Don't want to admit that my life is not what I dreamed of. Don't want to start from scratch again. They probably wouldn't even miss me. Could I risk that?

Together

We have been through a lot. I have often thought of leaving him. I have had enough many a time. I know he has felt the same. Every now and again we talk really honestly to each other. This has become easier over the years. I suppose when you stick together so long you feel stronger and have contemplated so many aspects of you relationship that nothing much surprises you. I know after our first kid was born we had many a desperate day. Both of us new to the job. Both of us exhausted and fed up of each other and the world. It is a wonder that we didn't split then. But then again I don't think either of us had the energy. Then as the little one got bigger we had more energy. But past wounds were welling up inside. Though we were desperate not to lose each other, dreading doing this job alone, sometimes we just couldn't stand the sight of the other. Usually I would avoid his eyes but if I caught sight of them all I could see was hate. It was like a reflection of what I felt inside. But there were so many problems, they never came out straight when we argued. I might have felt ugly and rejected and he might have felt isolated and excluded but we argued about money and him not taking responsibility. He felt he could never do anything right. I felt the exact same but for other reasons. Unhappy and struggling. No end to it. I think it was then that we started to spread our wings a bit. We started not depending on each other for all our happiness. I don't mean that we had affairs but we started meeting up with friends,

sometimes all together sometimes on our own. We
had something else to talk about. We had lives
besides the hum drum of each ordinary day. And as
we relaxed we could start to see all the great things
we had. We would dance again cheek to cheek
around the dining room. We could not only indulge
in our daughters bubbling energy but reflect it with
our own.

The second child arrived and we were a little more
prepared for the change. Even though she wasn't at
all like the first. We were easier on ourselves. We
knew we would survive. We may have been so on
the edge sometimes that we thought we would fall
off into an endless pit of despair but we kept on
going. Could laugh more in between and talk more
honestly. Yes, we have hurt each other over the
years. Mostly not intentionally. But though the scars
sometimes fester and ooze, most of the time we can
see beyond them and love each other for who we
are. Family life isn't easy in many ways but it is
enriching and I have got to know myself so much
more because of it. We are still together. We still get
excited by each other, every now and again. We are
kinder to each other and our expectations may be a
bit lower and more realistic. We are only human
after all. We arrived slightly damaged into our
relationship and try not to do too much damage to
each other now.

Stuck

Get a grip they would tell me. It has been a long while now. But for me time hasn't past. I put on my jacket, my boots and head for the door. I am going to visit him. I can talk to him, tell him what is going on in our lives. I get off the bus hoping no one will recognise me. I pull my hat down, not wanting to make eye contact with any one. I make my way into the graveyard. I spot a neighbour. I set off determined in the other direction hoping she hasn't seen me. We left this neighbourhood shortly after the accident. There were too many memories here. Our boy was in his teens, a big strapping boy. He headed off in the morning to school but never came home. Can you even imagine that? Don t, even the thought of it will rip you apart. My wife had had a baby shortly before. We were in the thick of it. Short nights, trying to cope with a teenager and daughter with learning difficulties but we were coping.
What can anyone say to us to comfort us? No words will make a difference. There is no compensation when you oldest son is ripped from you and you haven't even had a chance to say goodbye.
Worse than anything, is the not knowing what exactly happened. They were in the gym hall. He collapsed. Had he been pushed? All the kids were shocked too when he didn't wake up everybody presumed he was concussed and would wake up eventually. But he had no pulse, none at all. The police, the questions, the horror of it all, I still have nightmares.

Silent

I can't talk to anyone about my problems. I know my wife does. She has her group of pals and they meet up regularly. I have a few friends but we don't talk about how we feel. Maybe when our wives are with us we might express our opinion about personal things but otherwise we talk about sport or politics or situations that have arisen in the area. I would fell disloyal if I told people how I felt about my wife, my kids, my feelings. I can't always cope. I make lots of decisions. But it would be great to bounce my ideas against a good pal; someone neutral that wasn't emotionally involved in what's going on. Someone who would let me ramble on. Give their point of view. Share experience. Someone I could trust that wouldn't judge me for how I think, for my insecurities. Wouldn't think I was weak or most importantly wouldn't say something to others, blow things out of proportion. Someone that knows that you can be very much in love and still feel frustration, weariness, even bordering on hate sometimes. Often I see other men explode with anger about small things and I think to myself, there is probably a lot more behind that explosion then they would ever admit to. I get angry too and it comes out in the wrong way; in impatience, annoyance with mine and others stupidity. There is a deep well in me of so many things that I have never said to anyone. Sometimes it seeps out and spoils the day. The vessel is full. I can't talk to anyone and it is spilling out more and more.

Keeping to myself
It is a long time since my door bell rang. My telephone sits there still each day. I was never a great person for keeping in contact with others. There was almost so much else to do. I was busy. I wanted to get on with things. I couldn't bear the empty chitter chatter of small talk of the neighbours, the bitchy comments, the general nosiness. Work colleagues were pleasant and cooperative. I never quite seemed to understand what all the hype was about, about something imaginary on the television. I mean, what relevance did it have to our lives? I suppose you could say I have always been a bit of an outsider. I never did anything wrong, never annoyed anybody in particular. I just didn't quite fit in. I would smile absently when people babbled on pleasantly to me but was quite happy to get back to my office.
I half wanted to belong but thought they were all a bit stupid in a way. The things that interested them didn't interest me. I don't think they ever noticed my disdain. They probably thought I was just shy but their attempts to include me soon waned and I was relieved that I wouldn't have to sit through another event where I only felt awkward.
In many ways I am glad of the peace I have now. But I have got to wondering what life is all about. I never really achieved too much. But I am not a burden on society. I look after myself. Nobody would really know I am here.

My parents are dead and I have seldom contact with
the rest of my family. They have all families of their
own and are busy. It actually gives me an aching
feeling when I hear all the commotion in the
background when they do ring. I still don't belong. I
am still not sure if I want to. In fact I am not really
sure of anything anymore. I will just go take out the
rubbish now. Hopefully I won't bump in to one of
the neighbours.

Minds on shelves
Books, I love them. All those minds hidden in books
waiting to be explored. I pick one off the shelf in the
library and I don't know what I am letting myself in
for. I have had tough times in my life. One trip to the
library and I can enter into so many more lives more
exciting, funny or inspiring than mine. I can let free
of the troubles of my day. Sink into that other world.
Cry a little, laugh a little, immerse myself in another
zone.
I hated reading in school. I hated reading out loud. It
was torture all together. The first I learned of
reading out loud and not stuttering and tripping over
every word was when I read for my own child. I felt
animated. As she couldn't read, she didn't notice
when I got a word wrong or hesitated. She loved it
and her love of my stories kept me going. She was
excited to hear the next story and I was excited to
make all the animal noises and experience her glee.
I love to talk about books with the odd person I find
that likes the same types of books as me. There are
so many books out there it's not that often that I
meet someone that has read the same one. I often
write down the name of the books I love from the
library, buy my family and friends those books so
we can talk about them.
I remember years ago when I had never bought a
book for myself except a school book or a comic. I
was overwhelmed by the shelves of books. So many,
where would I start? The effort of choosing one. The
heat in the shops and the vastness of the packed

shelves making me faint. A good friend of mine bought me a book of short stories. Another good friend of mine took that book from me on a bus and started to read some of the stories to me aloud. I loved it. I wanted to read them myself. I finished that book and have kept it for old time's sake. The first of many that have filled my life, shaped my thoughts and opened my world to other ideas. Sometimes comforting me, knowing I am not alone in my thoughts, other times shocking me, realising there are so many people who don't think as I do. So many parallel worlds.

Rest

I have been looking forward to this day for a long time. I had loved working with all the people that were good colleagues but getting up every morning at the same time got tedious. The young ones coming out of university were always so quick to point out all the things that I didn't know, even though they had a lot to learn too.

Now I get up when I wake up, mostly before nine. I have time to walk down to the shop, get what I need for my lunch. Maybe take a ramble down the beach. I usually bump into one of my old croanies and we chat for a while. The sky there is fantastic. The salt air in my face wakes me up. I am happy in myself. I wander home and make my lunch. My wife is up and about and we chat a little. I have a good book out from the library. I just finish off my lunch and look forward to reading to my heart's content. There's a western on the telly after that I haven't seen for a while. I can watch that. There is certainly one advantage of not having the kids around. I get to look at what I want, when I want.

I am not a real social man but I enjoy a bit of company. The odd time an old pal rings and we meet up in the pub, have a few pints a bit of a chat and we head our own ways again. They had given us so many courses about how to manage our time once we had gone out on pension. What I really like about it is not managing my time. The nicest thing in the world is knowing that I do have time. Time to do what I want, when I want, with no pressure on. What could be more enjoyable than being master of your own time?

Next please
I have to move it seems. I kind of know it myself but
really I don't want to know. I know I am forgetful.
But some things are better to forget. My problem is I
don't forget my old memories. I forget that I put the
pan on with oil in it. Yes, it is embarrassing to admit
but that is what happened last week. I came back
into the kitchen and there was a flame leaping up out
of the pan. I might be old but I was quick acting. I
grabbed the tea cloth. Dampened it and threw it on
the pan. It was put out in a shot. I must say I was
shaking for a while afterwards. I really was caught
off guard. Off course I didn't mention anything to
my daughter. I didn't want her to be worried. But
she noticed the black stain on the ceiling above the
stove. I hadn't noticed it. And so I had to tell her.
Unfortunately there have been a few other incidents,
but nothing that important. I am getting old. I am not
my full self but I seem to be able to accept it more
than her.
She is afraid for me. But I am afraid that I will have
to give up my independence. I like the way my life
is. I am quite content to stay in bed longer in the
winter. Save on the heat. What would I want going
to an old folks home with all those strangers. All that
fussing around me. I want to be able to cook my
sausages the way I like them. I like to be able to eat
my bread pulling off the crusts first not having to
look over my shoulder to see who is looking.
I have had my day. I am ok with fading out. Even
dying doesn't threaten me as it used to but moving

from here does. Moving from where everything is familiar and cosy. Maybe it's a bit dirty and not so presentable, but that was never important to me and why should it be now.
I would rather die than move. But my heart keeps ticking. My mind is slowly going and my daughter is winning control.

Reversed roles

It doesn't seem that long ago since I was taking care of her. Getting her dinner on the table. Keeping the house nice and being a listening ear to all her stories. Now it is my turn.

I have been diagnosed with cancer. I haven't been well for some time. I haven't been quite myself.

I started on Chemo. The first dose didn't seem to take much out of me and so I decided to continue as my cancer cells were retreating. The battle had begun.

This lot of treatment didn't start as well. I got an infection from the infusion. I was lucky to survive that. My hair is gone. My nails are soft and my skin sore and cracked. I used to look in the mirror trying to fix myself up. I had been a quite a beautiful woman. My face had always been my strong point but even that is not the same. I see the aching in my eyes. my eyes welling up with tears. This cannot be life. This is so horrible. I will never be myself again. I don't want anyone to see me. Everything hurts even my gums when I eat. I don't want those dinners. I roll over and think I have to give this my best shot. My son and daughter are worn out visiting me. I see the worry etched on their faces. They reflect my haggard look. I really am doing my best. But I really have had enough. I am not sure that I want any more of this chemo. But what else can I do, give up and die?

Resurrection
I have my life back. You can't begin to imagine how
that is. I lost my hair. I lost my dignity. I was ready
to go but I just couldn't let go and now I am living.
Don't ask me how this happened. Don't ask the
doctors either they are not sure why either. I stopped
the chemo before it killed me altogether. It had been
enough. And though it has taken my system so long
to get back to normal, my scans are ok. I know that I
am not totally cured but I feel ok. I can get out and
walk. I can get my own dinner. I can laugh with my
friends and family. I am really alive. For too long I
hesitated. Thinking it can't be true. Afraid that each
scan would show that it was back in full force. I
have been living in fear every day. Losing my
appetite with the terror of taking things for granted.
But now 2 years on. I am learning to relax a bit. Live
each day. Live more and more. Till my body is tired
and tells me itself that it is time to say goodbye.
I want to laugh more, love more and eat more.

Escape
It takes me longer to pack my case the last few years
but I do it slowly over several weeks. The case is
open and I pop things into it as I think of them. I am
booked on a holiday with a travel group. It is great. I
have always loved travelling. I never know who will
be on the trip. We all just meet at the airport. It takes
a while for us all to get to know each other. But as
there are a few like me who are on their own and
some groups of pals who are quick to include me or
older married couples who are glad of a bit of
company it is never long till I feel right at home
among them.
I have never really talked about my family with
neighbours or friends. I never wanted to expose
them. But with these groups we all let our hair
down. We are able to talk so honestly. I never laugh
so much as on these trips. Laugh and feel accepted.
It is time out for us all.
I am lucky that I saved my money all those years.
Never squandered it on alcohol or cigarettes, like my
friends. We never had fancy holidays but now I can.
I love the thrill of sitting in that plane ready for
takeoff and not knowing what the next two weeks
will bring. My kids are all grown up now. My
husband is happy to look at the telly at home and I
am free to live out my old age having fun at least for
2 weeks.
I have explored so many countries now, seen so
much culture and history. I can understand so much
more of life. There are people from all over the

world on these trips, people like myself wanting to
see more than the inside of their houses.

Coping

Another number to strike out of my telephone book
The older I get the worse it is. The first was a shock,
the second even worse and it got worse and worse as
one by one they dropped off like flies and now the
time between the funerals is longer. There are not so
many of us left. We used to meet for a pint. We used
to meet on the beach or up in the village or even
bump into each other in the city. Now one by one I
can cross off their names in my telephone book.
Little by little I have less choice of pals. I am glad of
anyone to talk to. The telly is on all the time now. It
is difficult to motivate myself to get out of the chair.
Luckily enough I can still get around. Still get my
messages in the shops and cook my dinner. That all
takes time gives me something to do that I have
done for so many years and doesn't require much
thinking about.
I left the stove on yesterday and there was black
smoke coming from the grill pan when I came back
out to the kitchen. I will have to watch that I don't
forget that again. I could burn the place to the
ground.
I potter around get my stuff together. I realise I have
forgotten to get the milk in the shops. I have to go up
in the car.
I ease myself into the front seat. My back has been
killing me the last while. I know I am getting slower
to react and those bloody cars go so fast now on that
main road. They don't give you a minute.

I am tired, tired of trying, tired of doing the same old thing. I wouldn't mind if I popped off. I just don't want to drag on forever.

Another world
I was delivered in here in an emergency. I collapsed couldn't use my arm, couldn't speak. Now I am lying here in this bed all linked up to all these tubes and monitors. This is it. Is this what the rest of my life will be like? Not knowing what part of me will give up next. I was feeling fine. Actually better than I had felt in a long time. I can't understand it. I am sick of it. It is so frustrating to have to know that nothing is certain any more. Maybe nothing was ever certain but I felt I could rely on my body. I could know that it would do what I wanted. It was something I could control. I suppose that is the worst of things at the moment, the lack of control. The nice thing is that everybody makes a fuss. Everybody rallies round. Suddenly they all have time.
They will release me in a few days. I have to keep my injections more regular. I can't do what I want. I have to do what I am told like a school child. I am not sure I can deal with this. I will have to but what a drag. Why do we have to grow old? Somehow or other it doesn't seem as if my life ever started and now it is ending. The unknown. These trips to the hospital are tiring. Staying up half the night in casualty isn't what I would do to decrease stress but this is what you have to do to get a bed in this hospital.
This is a whole new world. One I am going to become familiar with, I suppose.

New generation
It's great to see them. See their bright faces. See the
health glowing in them. They make me laugh the
expressions on their faces, even when the little one
has her tantrums and roars and shouts. The noise
drives me mad but I have to grin. Seeing how she
wraps her way around her mam. Seeing how she can
turn on and off the charm.
I am lucky to have grandchildren. I didn't get to
enjoy my own children as much. I was off working.
I wasn't really into children; the noise, the energy of
them, the hard work. My wife did all that. I didn't
appreciate the work she put in. It is only when I see
my own daughter exhausted getting them all sorted
making sure they are fed, healthy and happy I realise
what a full time job it is.
I will never forget when my daughter came home
with her first baby. The little head, the velvet skin.
The perfect tiny fingers. Everything functioning and
beautiful. I nearly wept with joy. It overcame me,
the whole emotion of it. My little girl, a grown
woman now with her little baby. I could stare at the
little one for ever. She lit me up. As she got older
could talk run argue, I was so aware of her growth,
her intelligence. It fascinated me. Like looking at a
fascinating program on the television. But living it. I
never cease to me amazed at the wonder of her. The
wonder of human beings in general. Growing from
almost nothing. This little baby is getting big now.
She is almost a woman and she is my granddaughter.
She still makes me smile. I think she knows how

much I appreciate her. Maybe she can feel my adoration of the wonder of her. How come I never got to experience this earlier in life? Well I am just glad I got to live long enough to experience it now.

Waiting

I am lying here waiting. Waiting to die. But I want to hang on just a bit longer. My son has been back and forth across the water to me over the past year. But now it is time to say goodbye. I have battled with this cancer long enough now. I roared in frustration at the beginning. I am a big man. Well, I was a big man. I have shrunk beyond anything I could have imagined.

I have been lucky I have had a good life. I have had time to talk to all those I love. I have suffered and all those around me too. I can see it in their eyes as they look at me, the terror of seeing me change into this strange creature that they don't know. Those who have not witnessed the change over time are so shocked it registers on their faces and then they are so embarrassed as they know I see their shock. What can I do, I have to look at myself dwindling to nothing too. I have to see my arms that cut down trees and lifted boulders from my garden become stick like. I am fragile. My body is not doing what I want it to do. It has a mind of its own.

The acceptance is the hardest thing. It is what I have battled with the most. I have always been a fighter. Always found the solution to the problem, always known that if I hang on, things will get better. And now I have to let go.

But just one more hug. It breaks my heart to leave them all here. But I feel their sorrow and they see mine and now its goodbye.

Cold to the bone

How is it always so cold at funerals? I can't feel any heat at all. At least the sun is shining. We waited for you to die. Seeing you in pain ripped our family apart. Facing you leaving us divided our opinions. We all wanted the best for you. But each of us thought differently. But now you are gone. Nothing we could say or do can bring you back. I am numb, not feeling anything here. Standing here not believing it is you in that wooden box they are lowering into that freshly dug mud. How can I even allow myself to think it? I am exhausted from you dying. I could lie with you in that grave but I only want a rest.

I can't even cry. No tears come. I cry at films but this is something else. An emptiness, a hollowness fills me. I can't think of anything. Automatic mode. I don't want to leave you alone there. So very alone. At the same time I think you are going to turn around and hug me, appear out of nowhere. Not you who was dying in the bed last week but you who has always been there for me.

We had our tea afterwards. I shook so many hands. I smiled, even joked and spoke but I could hear myself from the inside. I am hiding inside here waiting for the pain to go away, waiting to come out again and everything to go on as normal.

And it does. The world does not stop for my sorrow. People nod and acknowledge my loss but they cannot feel it. I cannot feel it when I am rushing from one appointment to another and the kids are

flying around me asking for this and that. But as I lie
in bed at night, I lie there and feel the gnawing
loneliness.
I want to ring you, tell you what I have done today.
I know you are with me in so many ways in my
memories and things that surround me but I want a
hug and long warm, never ending hug.

Secrets

There is so much more to her life than we ever
imagined. It was only since her death that it has all
emerged. We were going though her papers trying to
make sense of her finances. Then we found her birth
certificate. It was only by chance that I really looked
at it and saw that she had another surname. Not the
maiden name that we knew her to have. Not the
name of our grandparents but another totally
different. The birthday tallied though. So I
rummaged further and found more photos and
details of people we had never heard of.

I decided to look into it further and found out that
she had been adopted at an early age. She had never
sought contact with her real mother. It had not
always been possible.

And so I asked the rest of my family what they
thought of the situation. My oldest brother had
thought that he had once heard mention that she had
been adopted but wasn't so sure.

We decided to contact the original family through
the adoption bureau. We were astounded to find out
that she had lived so close to them, in the same
village. She had even attended the same school as
her other sisters and brothers.

Had my mother known? I don't think it was
possible. Why did she keep it secret from us? Maybe
she was happy enough as she was and didn't want to
delve into the past.

We would have loved to have known more. Talk to
her find out how she felt? Would it not have been

wonderful for her to see her blood relations? Or maybe it would have brought her more pain. We will never know. Her own mother is long dead we will never know what situation she was in that made her give up her child. Although my mother seemed to be happy enough I wonder how her mother had felt all those years seeing her girl grow up so close and never being able to hug her.

Not alone
It could have been a dream. But it doesn't matter
what it was it has helped me so much. He stood
there in my room a short distance from my bed and
told me to relax he would take care of everything.
My mother was dying of cancer. She had so much
unfinished business. He was her father. He knew her
well. They had been very close and he was very
special to me. He only lived till I was 4 but he let me
dance on his toes in the dining room. He was a big
man. I laughed and felt loved. I had not thought of
him for so many years. But he is still around, still
there when I most need him. He is still looking after
his family in his own way. Thank you.

Afterword

I noticed while collecting the information from people from all walks of life that although the list of the good memories was usually longer than the list of the bad memories. The bad memories seem to affect the person in a lasting way. Maybe those memories which broke our trust in mankind and have made us more afraid serve to protect us in the future. But it is of no use to us if it makes us so afraid that we cannot live our lives at all.

I wish each person the courage to live their lives to the full, to discover their full potential and that their potential will hopefully be to the benefit of the people around them and themselves.

Good luck on your journey.

If you feel like writing down your memories, there are enough blank spaces in the book for you to start. When you are having a bad day it is always good to look back at your list of good memories (like taking out old photographs). It is also interesting to see if you have learned anything good from your bad memories – maybe even remembering people who helped you out during that time.

Reaching out to each other makes the difference that turns bad memories into good ones.